Praise for *Can You See Me?*

Also by Libby Scott and Rebecca Westcott:

Can You See Me?
Do You Know Me?

LIBBY SCOTT & REBECCA WESTCOTT

WAYS

to

BE

me

SCHOLASTIC

Published in the UK by Scholastic, 2021
Euston House, 24 Eversholt Street, London, NW1 1DB
Scholastic Ireland, 89E Lagan Road, Dublin Industrial Estate,
Glasnevin, Dublin, D11 HP5F

SCHOLASTIC and associated logos are trademarks and/or
registered trademarks of Scholastic Inc.

Text © Libby Scott and Rebecca Westcott, 2021
Cover lettering by Aaron Cushley, 2021

The rights of Libby Scott and Rebecca Westcott to be identified as the authors of this
work have been asserted by them under the Copyright, Designs and Patents Act 1988.

ISBN 978 0702 30835 2

A CIP catalogue record for this book is available from the British Library.

Printed by CPI Group (UK) Ltd, Croydon, CR0 4YY
Paper made from wood grown in sustainable forests
and other controlled sources.

1 3 5 7 9 10 8 6 4 2

To Marnie and Frankie, thank you for letting me be your big sister.

To Louie, who unlocked the love I never thought I could feel again for another dog.

Libby

For everyone doing their best to figure out who they are.

Rebecca

PROLOGUE

Three words.

Imagine that's all you've been given to describe yourself. What would you choose?

Loud, tall, arty?

Quiet, small, sporty?

Or perhaps you'd go a little further and really think about what makes you *you*.

Loyal, kind, brave?

Funny, honest, hard-working?

Or, maybe you'd take a really long look at the person you are and go even deeper.

Impulsive, determined, principled?

Solitary, unpredictable, curious?

If Tally Olivia Adams were asked to describe herself in just three words, she'd have somewhat of a problem.

In fact, she would struggle if she were allowed five words or ten words or even the huge classroom dictionary that sits on Miss Balogun's desk.

She could possess all the words in the world, but it wouldn't help. Because it's almost impossible to describe yourself when you haven't figured out who you are yet.

ALL ABOUT ME

NAME: Natalia Adams (but everyone calls me Tally)
AGE: Ten years old

THINGS I AM GOOD AT:

1. I can speak Spanish (a bit, anyway).

2. I'm pretty good on my skateboard even if I do sometimes fall off.

3. I've taught myself to play Taylor Swift songs on the ukulele and I can sing really high notes, which will be good if I ever need to communicate with a dolphin.

4. I can also hold my breath underwater for one whole minute.

THINGS I AM BAD AT:

1. Being interrupted, especially by my horrible big sister Nell, who hardly lets me say two words without shouting over me.

2. Making mistakes. I mean, don't get me wrong – I make mistakes all the time. But I hate it and I'll do anything not to get something wrong which often means that I won't even try something, just in case I mess it up. Making mistakes makes me feel horrible inside.

3. Being told what to do – which is hard when I have to go to school because that's all that teachers seem to want to do all day. They tell me where I have to sit and when I'm allowed to talk and even what colours I have to use when painting a tree (apparently blue isn't OK – try telling Picasso that!).

CHAPTER 1

It's all Granny Lola's fault. If she had never created her so-called *famous* recipe, then there's a chance that Tally's day might have improved. A *tiny* chance, but a chance all the same. But the steaming portion of beef chilli that Mum has just placed in front of her has put an end to any hope that today is going to end well.

"No." Tally drops her head and stares at the table. "I can't eat that."

Mum sits down next to Dad, who gives a big sigh.

"Don't start, Tally. Not today."

Mum pats him on the arm in the same way that she does when she's trying to tell him to stop talking, and then looks at Tally with her special *I am very calm* smile plastered to her face.

"Nobody's starting anything. I've got a lot on my plate

1

right now, and I just want us all to enjoy the nice meal that I've cooked and have a peaceful evening."

Tally narrows her eyes and scowls. Mum isn't the only one with a lot on her plate – there's so much beef chilli on Tally's plate that it's almost oozing over the sides. Which is disgusting, and also one of the problems.

Not that Mum is going to listen to her.

"How was your visit to the gallery?" asks Dad, scooping up some rice. Tally watches as a few of the grains drop from the fork and land in the chilli sauce where they float like tiny maggots.

Mum nods. "It was good, actually. They want to take two of my larger canvases and eight of the smaller ones, so I'm going to be busy for the next few weeks." She looks across the table at Tally and Nell. "You two are going to have to help out a bit more around the house while I get my paintings finished. I'm going to need you to sort the laundry and a few other things."

Nell makes a grunting sound. "Well, I've got a ton of homework due in, and you already said that I could stay over at Rosa's house this weekend." She jerks her head towards Tally. "She'll have to do some chores for a change."

Tally blinks as everything seems to change colour, as

2

if someone has just taken the lid off one of Mum's paint pots and thrown it wildly around the room. She tries to see past the red mist that clouds the air for her.

"I'm sure we're all happy to do our bit," Dad tells Nell pointedly. "Especially if we want a lift to Rosa's house on Saturday."

Tally's shoulders relax and she leans back in her chair, balancing on the back two legs. She has no intention of touching anyone's dirty pants and socks, but it's OK because she most definitely does not want to go to Rosa's house at the weekend, so she doesn't need to do any chores.

"Don't rock on your chair," says Mum, automatically. "And eat up. We've got blackberry crumble for pudding."

"I can't eat it," Tally tells her, wobbling precariously on the chair. "I already told you."

Mum slowly and deliberately puts her fork down on to the plate, and even though it hardly makes a sound, in Tally's head it's as loud as a gunshot.

"I spent ages making this and you're going to eat it."

Tally slams the chair legs down and glares at Mum. "I *can't*."

"Oh, deepest joy," drawls Nell in the irritating voice that she woke up with on her fourteenth birthday last month. "Another wonderful Adams family mealtime where Tally has a strop and makes everything about her."

Tally can feel her heart pounding, as if she's running a race and not sitting quietly in the kitchen. "I do *not* make everything about me! Nothing is ever about me, actually. If it was then I wouldn't be forced to eat disgusting food that I hate."

"Don't be so rude, Tally," says Dad. "And you love Granny Lola's famous beef chilli. We had it a couple of weeks ago and you ate it then."

"It was right last time, but it isn't right today!" Tally closes her eyes and tries to find the words, but they just won't come. Instead of words, all she can see is pictures: snapshots of the day running through her head like a film reel.

Stepping in a puddle on the way to school.

Horrible Luke calling her rude names at break-time.

The way the noise in the school hall bounced off the walls and straight into her ears at lunchtime.

"Well, it's the same meal that it was *before*," Mum informs her, and when Tally opens her eyes she can see that Mum's special smile has got even bigger. "But it's your choice. You can eat your meal and then have some lovely crumble, or you can choose *not* to eat it and *not* have any pudding."

Tally takes a deep breath and tries to stay calm, but it's impossible when Mum has said something so monumentally ridiculous. It's not Mum's fault, Tally knows that – but it still hurts every time she tries to use one of the ridiculous strategies that she and Dad learnt on the useless parenting course they went on last year. Nell said that they should have sent Tally on a *How to Be a Better Kid* course instead, and even though Mum told her off for being unkind, Tally is pretty sure that both her parents agreed with her. Anyway, the parenting course wasn't very good, because the only thing they seemed to learn was how to make things even worse by pretending that Tally has choices when really they're offering her a choice between *everything*, including something that she can't eat, or literally *nothing*, including the one thing that she *can* eat. They're trying to make her choose between two horrible things, which isn't a real choice at all.

Tally hears Dad ask Nell a question about school, and for a few minutes the kitchen is filled with the sound of Nell's long, boring speech about the demands of year nine and how she really, really needs a laptop, and *blah blah blah* and *me, me, me*. Tally stops listening and stares at her plate. The beef chilli lurks menacingly in front of her, the kidney beans all slimy and soft, and she gulps, trying to swallow the lump that has appeared in her throat. What Mum and Dad said is true – she *did* eat this meal a few weeks ago, and it *is* the same meal that it was before.

But she could cope with it last time. She can't cope today. And there is no way that she can eat it. She extends one finger and pushes the plate, just a tiny bit.

"I only want to eat the crumble," she says quietly.

"No chilli, no crumble," says Dad.

The plate moves a little further.

"Just eat it," snaps Mum, apparently forgetting that she is trying to be the *calm parent*. "I haven't got time for this."

Tally's hand twitches.

"Can we please get back to talking about my new laptop?" whines Nell. "And not Tally's latest fussy food fad. God – I'm glad Rosa didn't come for supper tonight. Her little sister is really cute – not a brat like Tally. She'd think you're a right pain if she was here."

And then she yelps as Granny Lola's famous beef chilli lands on the floor, splashing tomato sauce all over her socks.

"I'm not being fussy and I'm not a brat!" screeches Tally. "And I don't care what other people think!"

"Tally!" Mum and Dad shout in unison, staring at the horror before them. "What on earth is wrong with you?"

The horror pushes her chair back and heads to the back door, ripping it open and then hurtling down the garden path to the safety of her den under the willow tree.

"There's nothing wrong with me, is there?" she mutters, picking up her favourite soft toy, who was left there to guard her secret space when Mum called her in for tea. "Except that my feet were wet and scratchy all day and I couldn't eat my yoghurt because I didn't have a spoon and it was too noisy to think properly and people are mean."

She hugs Billy tightly and gazes at his face. "Why does nothing ever work out for me?"

The teddy bear stares back at her sympathetically through its one remaining button eye, but he hasn't got the words to explain it any more than Tally does. He has to agree, though.

Everything does seem to end up going wrong when Tally is involved.

TALLY'S LOVE / HATE LIST

SOME THINGS I HATE ARE:
Change
Labels
Seams in socks
Wearing a coat
Soggy cereal
Loud noises
School
Jokes I don't get
Being told to do things – anything in fact
Being embarrassed in front of others
Having to stop doing something I'm enjoying

SOME OF MY FAVOURITE THINGS ARE:
Taylor Swift
The sound of rain (and the smell, actually)
The smell of stables
My fluffy slippers
The words "I don't see why not"
Dogs and horses
Taylor Swift again
Music, but only my music – well, only Taylor Swift, really

CHAPTER 2

The instant Tally steps out of the car, everything hits her at once. The smell of the hay, the sounds of hooves coming from the other side of the yard, and best of all, the sight right in front of her.

"Can you believe that we're doing this?" squeals Layla, standing beside her. "I couldn't go to sleep last night because I was so excited."

Tally looks around, trying to take it all in.

"This is so much better than chocolate," she sighs.

Layla's mum grins at Tally's mum.

"That's quite the endorsement," she laughs. "I'm not sure that I think there's *anything* better than chocolate!"

Tally steps forward, towards the fence that separates them from the horses.

"I would never eat chocolate again if it meant that I could keep coming here."

Mum puts a hand on her shoulder. "This is a one-off visit," she reminds her, for the millionth time. "An Easter gift instead of a chocolate egg."

Layla's mum sniffs loudly. "I could have bought *two hundred* eggs for the price of this little jaunt," she says.

But neither Layla nor Tally is listening. The main door to the stables has just opened, and a woman in riding boots is striding towards them.

"Are you my ten o'clock lesson?" she barks, jerking a chin at their mothers. "I'm Ginny. You may as well leave them here and come back in two hours. It's far too cold to stand out here waiting, and I don't want you cluttering up my tack room."

Mum throws Tally a quick look. "Do you want me to wait in the car?" she asks quietly.

"Off you go," replies the woman before Tally can answer. "Best if you both go and get a coffee and let the kids get on with it." Then she turns to face the girls and gives them a long look as if she's trying to figure something out. "Hmmm. I think we'll put you on Shadow," she says, to Layla. "And as for you…" She stares hard at Tally's face. "Yes. You'll be perfect for Peaches. She's spirited, like you."

Tally breathes out in relief. She doesn't know why, but she very much wants to impress this slightly snappy Ginny-woman, and it feels like she just passed some kind of test. Without checking to see if they're following her, Ginny spins on her heel and marches back to the stables. Tally glances at Mum. They'd agreed that Mum would stay and watch. Doing this without her nearby was not part of the plan.

Tally swallows hard. She could make a fuss and demand that Mum be allowed to stay, but that would take time – precious time she could be using to meet Peaches. For a brief minute, she can feel tears prickle behind her eyes, and she wonders why even the nicest and best things always have to be so hard.

"Let's go!" says Layla, grabbing hold of Tally's hand. "The horses are waiting for us!"

It's true. And Tally has been waiting for this day for so, so long.

"I'll be here when you finish the lesson," Mum tells her. "I can't wait to hear about how you get on!"

Layla starts to walk towards the stables, tugging Tally behind her. There is just time to wave goodbye to

Mum before they're inside, and the outside world and everything in it immediately vanishes from Tally's sight and her thoughts.

It's warm inside the stables, and Tally can hear a soft whinnying coming from some of the stalls. The air smells grass-green and dandelion-yellow, and she inhales deeply, filling her lungs with the comforting scent. It feels like home, even though she's never been here before.

"This is Saira," Ginny tells Layla, as a teenage girl walks up to them. "She'll show you what to with Shadow and make sure that you're doing everything safely."

"Hi," says Saira. "Shall we go and meet Shadow, then? She's a total darling and a sweetheart. and you're going to love her!"

Layla beams excitedly at Tally and then follows Saira into a nearby stall. Ginny picks up a bucket and some brushes and starts heading towards the far end of the stables, while Tally pauses, unsure about what she should be doing.

"Hurry up, then," calls Ginny, without breaking her stride. "If you're coming."

Tally dashes after her and reaches her side just as Ginny pulls aside the gate to the end stall.

"Is Peaches a *total darling* too?" she asks, panting for

breath. "Am I going to love her?"

Ginny makes a snorting noise that sounds a little bit like it might have come from the horse that is standing in front of them.

"I'm not sure that anyone would call you a *total darling*, would they?" she says, rubbing her hands on the horse's flank. "You're far too fiery for that. Now, are you coming in to help or not?"

Tally hesitates. "I'm not sure. Why have you given me a fiery horse and not a *sweetheart* like Layla?"

Ginny raises one eyebrow. "Because I thought you'd be good for her," she says firmly. "And just maybe, she might be good for you. There's nothing wrong with being fiery, you know. As long as it's for a good reason."

Tally thinks for a moment and then steps inside the stall.

Ginny nods. "Close the stable door behind you," she orders. "And I'll show you how to give her coat a proper brushing." She hands Tally a large brush and then, taking a slightly smaller one in her own hands, she starts sweeping it across the horse's body in broad, circular strokes. "Copy what I do."

As gently as she possibly can, Tally puts the brush on Peaches' side.

"I hope this doesn't hurt you," she whispers, slowly moving it in a circle. Hair brushing is one of Tally's least favourite things to do.

"It doesn't hurt her at all." Ginny is watching Tally's every move. "You're making sure that she doesn't have any dirt or grit that might irritate her skin, and it's also a chance to check that she doesn't have any injuries. Grooming a horse properly is part of showing that you care about it. You can give her nose a rub now and introduce yourself."

Ginny moves around to the back of the horse, and Tally takes a few steps until she's standing in front of Peaches' face. She doesn't know how she's supposed to introduce herself to a horse, and she can feel herself starting to get nervous, so she does what she always does at school when things are awkward and throws herself head first into a performance.

"Hi," she says, making her voice bright and perky. "So – I'm Tally. I'm ten years old and my star sign is Cancer, which means that I'm hardworking and loyal and highly imaginative, but that I can also be a bit moody and difficult to get to know."

"The two of you should get along well, then." Ginny's voice floats up from somewhere in the region of the horse's backside. "Keep going – I'm enjoying this."

Tally swells with pride. "I'm not sure how tall I am, but on the height chart in our kitchen it says that I'm the same height as a walrus when it's sitting up, which I think is quite cool although I don't look anything like a walrus. And I'm one centimetre taller than the height restriction for the World's Second Fastest Roller-coaster, which is brilliant because I really love roller-coasters, and if I ever to get to visit America then I'd be really sad if I couldn't go on it because I'm too small."

She pauses to take a quick breath and Peaches nudges her nose against Tally's arm. Tally giggles and runs her hand over the horse's nose.

"She likes you," states Ginny, emerging from the other side of the stall. "And she doesn't like everyone. Not everyone understands her or sees her for who she really is."

"That's the same for me," confesses Tally. "It's probably the same for you too. I bet you get misunderstood all the time and people think you're a bit grumpy when really you're actually quite nice."

Ginny nods seriously, although her mouth is twitching at the sides.

"It is," she agrees. "But when you find someone who

does see you, then it's extra special. Now – enough chitter-chatter. You're here to work, not have a tea party."

Together they finish brushing Peaches down, and when every inch of her is shining, Ginny takes Tally out of the stall and over to a small table covered with riding hats. They find one that fits, and even though it feels heavy and uncomfortable and just awful under Tally's chin, she doesn't say a word.

"You're all set," says Ginny, giving her an approving look. "Go and stand with your friend by the main doors and we'll bring the horses out. Peaches is going to want to trot, but if you give her clear, firm instructions then she'll walk slowly for you. And that's how she'll show you that *she* cares."

Tally scampers across the stable floor to where Layla is already waiting.

"This is the best!" calls Layla as she approaches. "My horse is so sweet and cute and adorable – I love her so much!"

Tally steps to one side as Ginny leads Peaches through the doors. As they pass, Peaches gives a loud snort as if she's heard Layla's proclamation of love for Shadow and is unimpressed.

Layla's face screws up in sympathy. "Oh, bad luck,

Tally. Your horse is nowhere near as lovable as mine."

Tally shakes her head at her friend. "She might not be sweet," she tells her. "But that doesn't mean that she isn't lovable. And anyway, I'd rather be fiery than cute."

And then she walks across the yard to the mounting block, where Ginny is waiting to help her get up on to Peaches and settle herself in the saddle. When her feet are securely in the stirrups, Ginny shows her how to let Peaches know that she needs to walk slowly.

"You have to be firm but gentle," she tells Tally. "If you feel her wanting to go faster, then the first thing you must do is to breathe out, loudly and slowly. That will tell her that you want something from her and give her some advance warning. Nobody likes abrupt demands being made of them, after all."

Tally definitely agrees with this. She hates it if Mum or Dad suddenly yell instructions at her – it makes her head feel fuzzy.

"Then you can say the word 'walk' in a very calm voice," continues Ginny. "If you sound panicked then Peaches will get panicked because she needs to know that you have the control and that she can trust you."

Tally understands. There is nothing more frightening than knowing that the person who is supposed to be in charge is feeling out of their depth.

"The important thing with horses and misbehaviour," Ginny says, handing a set of reins to Tally, "is to identify whether they *can't* do as you ask or they *don't want to* do as you ask. They're two very different things, but we can help the horse to do the right thing by being patient and relaxed, and by never, ever punishing. It's far better to give rewards for hard work than to punish for getting something wrong."

Tally nods enthusiastically. Sometimes, people ask her to do things that she just *can't* do, even though they aren't things that other people think are particularly tricky. She knows exactly what *can't* feels like – it's like having your tummy filled up with wriggling, squirming snakes while your head explodes with tiny fireworks. *Can't* is the scariest feeling in the whole world, especially when everyone else thinks that it's really *won't*.

After double-checking that everything is as it should be, Ginny picks up the rope and leads them forward into the training paddock, where they walk round and round in circles. Tally and Layla wave energetically at each other as they pass, Layla on the docile, plodding Shadow, and Tally on the lively Peaches who, despite her desires to run like the wind, walks calmly and slowly for the girl perched on her back, who whispers and reassures and praises the horse for following her instructions.

And even though they're only walking in circles, it seems to Tally that, with every step that Peaches takes, they are going on a journey together. One that she will never forget.

WHY HORSES ARE THE BEST

1. The smells – sweet, earthy, animally. I could smell that all day and never feel disgusted!

2. The sounds – horses' hooves. There is no sound more soothing or thrilling in the world.

3. The feeling – slight butterflies at first, and then as I relaxed, this lovely feeling of rhythm, like me and Peaches turned into one thing instead of two separate ones.

4. I never had to try to explain anything to her, she just knew and understood my signals. If only humans could be like that with me – just understand me without me having to fully explain and argue for everything!

5. I wish that I could feel like that all the time.

CHAPTER 3

"Shall we play our game again at break-time?"

Tally glances at the front of the class as she speaks, checking that Miss Balogun isn't looking her way, but the teacher is busy trying to coax the whiteboard screen into turning on.

Layla turns and grins at her best friend. "Yeah! I was thinking that Shadow and Peaches could be competing in a dressage competition, and everything is going well until Peaches stumbles and Shadow has to take her place."

Tally opens her mouth, but before she can say anything Miss Balogun moves to the front of the room and raises her hand into the air. Everyone stops talking and the classroom falls silent. Tally pulls her newest pencil case towards her and checks that everything is in its proper place. She got this one at the weekend after begging Mum to buy it for her. Mum wasn't that happy about it because she said that Tally already has seven pencil cases, and nobody needs that many. She gave in though, after Tally pointed out that she didn't have one like *this*, with little sections for the ruler and rubber and pens, and that a pencil case like this one would make it so much easier for her to get her work done.

"We're nearly at the end of the lesson," Miss Balogun informs them. "Anyone who has completed up to question eight may go out to play. Anyone who has chosen to spend their learning time *unwisely* ..." She eyes a few members of year six and tilts her head at them. "... will have to stay in until the work is done. You've got five minutes to make up for any wasted time, and I strongly suggest that you use it."

Twenty-nine heads hastily bend over their books, and for a few minutes the only sound in the room is the scratching of pens on paper. Tally blinks hard and tries to make her eyes focus on the questions, but it's impossible now that Miss Balogun has given them a deadline. All she can see is the clock on the classroom wall, ticking faster and faster as time runs out. She can't miss her break, not when Layla has agreed to play their game. Well, she calls it *their* game, but it's hers really. She made it up after their riding lesson, and while it's in no way as good as the real thing, it helps to keep the amazing memory of her time with Peaches fresh in her head. Plus, she always has the best ideas, and she knows the most about horses. Layla is the best friend ever, but she doesn't always get it right. Like what she just said about Peaches stumbling in the dressage competition. There is no way that Peaches would ever stumble. Tally guides her too well to ever allow her to fall.

"OK. If you've finished question eight then you can leave your book open on the desk and go out to play," announces Miss Balogun. "Don't forget to take a coat – it's still only March and it's cold. That applies to you too, Miles."

On the other side of the room, Miles gives Miss Balogun the thumbs-up sign and then goes back to flicking his index finger against his thumb, which is what he always does whenever he hasn't got something in his hands. He's dressed in shorts and a T-shirt, and Tally doesn't think she's ever seen him wearing anything else other than on school photograph day in year four when the teacher insisted that he put on a jumper so that he'd look the same as everyone else. Miles tugged it off the instant that the photo was taken and shoved it in the back of his tray, where it has presumably stayed ever since. Miss Balogun can make him *take* a coat outside, but she can't make him *put it on,* and they both know it. Tally thinks that Miss Balogun reminds him every day just to make herself feel better.

Miles doesn't seem to care that he dresses differently. In fact, there are quite a few things about Miles that are different to the other kids, but it doesn't seem to bother him, which Tally finds hard to understand. Not when the most important thing about being in year six is fitting in with everyone else, which is harder than Tally ever thought it could be.

Layla pushes her chair back. "Are you coming?" she asks, pulling her snack out of her desk drawer.

Tally shakes her head. "I haven't even started question seven," she mutters. "I'm never going to get it finished before the end of break."

Layla leans over the desk and points at the page.

"The answer to question seven is right there," she whispers, pointing at the reading comprehension that they've been studying. "The boy decides to take the old rowing boat to explore the island. And question eight is about the weird statue that he finds – just write down that it was to do with his ancestors or something. I'll wait for you outside, so hurry up, OK?"

Tally gives her a grateful smile and starts to write. The classroom empties and it's quite peaceful with just her and Miss Balogun in the room. She scrawls her answers on to the page, finding it easier to work without everyone else around her, and then shoves her hand in the air to get the teacher's attention.

"Are you finished?" Miss Balogun walks across to Tally's desk and casts her eyes across the book. "Off you go, then."

Tally springs from her seat and speeds towards the door.

"Oh, and Tally?" Miss Balogun's voice holds her back. "Next time, try to focus on the work and not on having a chat with Layla."

Tally feels her cheeks flaming bright red, but she manages to nod before hurtling out of the room and down the stairs. She *was* focused on the work. Mostly, anyway. As focused as a person can be when they're surrounded by constant noise and weird year six smells and sitting on the world's most uncomfortable chair and, on top of all that, trying not to think about the argument they might have had with their mum that morning when their horrible big sister ate the last of the cereal and didn't even say sorry.

She pushes through the door at the bottom of the stairs and out into the biting March air, dashing past Miles, who is sitting on the ground engrossed in the latest edition of the *Guinness Book Of World Records*, which is the only book Tally has ever seen him read. In her hurry to get outside she's forgotten her coat, but it doesn't matter because Layla is waiting for her, and she's got the best idea for a story about Peaches rescuing Shadow from a crumbling cliff edge and impending doom.

"Tally! Over here!"

Layla's voice cuts through the screams and yells of the playground, and Tally starts to walk across to where she's standing with some of the other year six girls, ducking to dodge an airborne football as she goes.

"You're here!" calls Layla, pulling away from Lucy and Ayesha and waving madly at Tally. "Come on, you're on our team!"

Tally stares at her best friend. "You said that we could play our game."

"Well, yes but…"

"We've already started playing Dodge," interrupts Lucy. "And it's our turn to run, so come and line up. The boys are already in position."

Tally's hands start to tingle, which is something that happens when she gets upset or worried. There's only one way to get rid of this feeling once it starts, and that is to flap her hands until she's flapped out all of the fizziness, but she can't do that at school.

So she folds her arms across her chest and pins her hands under her elbows where they can't do anything embarrassing. "You said that we could play *our* game," she says to Layla. "You promised."

"Don't have a go at Layla," says Ayesha. "You weren't even out here. Honestly, Tally – why do you have to always make everything so difficult?"

Tally feels her blood start thumping in her veins, the way it always does when something completely unfair happens. It wasn't her fault that she wasn't outside at the start of break; she'd have totally got the work finished if Miss Balogun hadn't distracted her with her stupid deadline and countdown. And now it's all starting to go wrong and she can feel the other girls' attention drifting away from her.

"OK, OK." Tally starts to jiggle on the spot. "In that case, how about a performance of *The Tally Show*? We haven't had one for ages and I reckon it's about time for Marjorie to make a surprise appearance."

27

She bends forward, one hand on her hip and puts on her best old-lady voice.

"*Ooh, love – you might have given me a bit of warning, you know? This dodgy hip means that I can't just leap into an impromptu performance whenever you feel like it.*"

Tally straightens up and spins round to look the other way as if she's having a conversation with old-lady Marjorie.

"Come off it, Marjorie. It's not like you had anything better to be doing, is it?"

"Not this again," mutters Ayesha, shaking her head.

"*I'll have you know that I was very busy,*" rasps Marjorie, seemingly unbothered by Ayesha's disapproval. "*I was down at the bingo with the girls, eating my Digestive biscuits. Ooh, I do love a Digestive biscuit! Anyway, I was two numbers away from calling Housey-Housey. I just needed a Sweet Sixteen, Never Been Kissed and a number forty-four, Droopy Drawers.*"

"What's the weirdo doing now?" calls Luke, who's somehow suddenly right there.

"Marjorie!" gasps Tally, blocking him out. "This is a school! You can't go around saying things like *Droopy Drawers* here."

Marjorie gives her best old-lady cackle. "*I've said it*

before and I'll say it again. You young people are just a bunch of snowflakes."

She turns and grins at the girls. "Who do you want to see next? I can do Angry Des or Irritable Maureen. You can choose!"

"Just stop it," mutters Lucy, glancing worriedly around. "You're being really embarrassing."

"Tally." Layla steps forward. "I've already started playing Dodge. Let's play this game now, and then we can play the other game at lunchtime, OK?"

The Tally Show disappears into thin air, as quickly as it arrived.

No. It is *not* OK.

Not even a tiny bit.

Layla agreed that they could play their game, and best friends shouldn't go back on their word.

Tally shakes her head. "It won't be the same at lunchtime. We have to play now."

Layla looks at Lucy and Ayesha. "Could we switch games?" she asks them. "Just for a bit? Tally does have brilliant ideas and it'll be really fun."

Lucy tilts her head to the side. "Aren't we a bit old to be pretending that—"

"Are you playing or not?" shouts Luke. "Or are you girls

worried that we're going to be faster than you? If you've got Weirdo Adams on your team, then you're definitely going to lose!"

Tally's stomach twists and she clenches her fists. Luke never used to bother her, but ever since they started in year six, he's been getting worse and worse, calling her nasty names and sniggering behind his hand when she walks into the classroom. Some of the other kids have started doing it too, although never when Miss Balogun might catch them.

"Shut up!" bellows Layla, always loyal. "You're weird too!"

For some reason this doesn't make Tally feel any better.

"And you *wish* that you were faster than us!" yells Lucy before turning back to face Tally. "We *have* to play Dodge now," she says. "Otherwise they'll think we're chicken and we'll have to listen to them bragging about how great they are for the rest of the day."

Ayesha nods. "We definitely have to play."

"I don't want to play that stupid game," snaps Tally. "I want us all to play *my* game for a change. My game is better."

Lucy frowns. "You're not in charge," she points out. "And you can't tell us what to do."

"Yeah, stop being so bossy," adds Ayesha, linking arms with Lucy. "We don't want to play that silly horse game. We're not babies."

"I'm *not* bossy and it's *not* a silly horse game!" Tally's voice is loud, louder than she meant it to be. "You're being horrible and I don't know what your problem is."

Lucy rolls her eyes at Ayesha. "We aren't the ones with the problem," she tells Tally. Then she turns to Layla. "You can choose. Either come and play Dodge with all of us or stay here and play *horsey horsey*."

Ayesha laughs as the two girls head towards the painted line that is used as the starting position for Dodge. Layla puts her hand on Tally's arm.

"They didn't mean to be unkind," she says.

Tally shrugs her off. "Yes they did! They said that my game was for babies, which is the most stupid thing I've ever heard."

Layla sighs quietly. "Not everyone sees things the way that you do, Tally. Other people don't want to play imaginary games now that we're in year six, but that's OK. It's OK to be different."

Tally looks at her and then turns and walks away. She's had enough of listening to other people say ridiculous things. There's nothing different about her, and she's pretty sure she sees things exactly the same way that she always has done, even if it does feel like every time she opens her mouth lately, someone gets annoyed or upset with her.

Layla is right about one thing though. The rest of the class seems to have changed since they started in year six, and nothing is the same. Nobody wants to play the same games that they've always played or laugh about the same stuff that they've always laughed about, and when she tries to join in their conversations, it sometimes feels like they've all learnt a new language and nobody remembered to tell her. She feels constantly on the outside and never, ever good enough.

And if things are different then it's everyone else who has changed, not her.

COPING WITH SCHOOL QUIZ

1. You plan to play a game at break-time with your best friend, but then everything changes and everyone wants you to play another game instead. Do you:

A. Smile and agree to join in, pleased to be included?
B. Feel a bit fed up but suck it up and join in anyway?
C. Thank them but say you don't really feel like playing their game today, and then go to find someone else to hang out with?
D. Make everyone think that you're sulking because you didn't get your own way when really you're trying not to cry because this wasn't the plan?

ANSWER: Definitely D. I was so set on Layla and I playing the horse game, and once I have something set in my mind it's not just a bit hard for me to change direction, it's actually impossible. It's like I have glue sticking the idea to the inside of my brain and no matter how hard I try I just can't shift the thought.

2. You're sitting in class watching something on the screen and it suddenly gets really loud. Do you:

A. Laugh and shout like everyone else?

B. Not even notice?

C. Wince a bit but wait for the teacher to turn down the volume?

D. Slam your hands over your ears, desperately trying to block out the sound?

ANSWER: D again. Loud noises really hurt my ears and make it difficult for me to think properly.

3. One of your friends tells a joke and everyone starts laughing but you don't see what's so funny. Do you:

A. Laugh anyway, just so nobody thinks that you're stupid?

B. Say "What? I don't get it?" for about the fifteenth time that day?

C. Tell an even funnier joke that you DO get?

ANSWER: Actually, I do all three of these. Which one just depends on what kind of day it is. If I'm feeling tired and a bit stressed out, then I'll just laugh along – but I usually end up laughing too hard and then everyone knows that I didn't get the joke anyway.

CHAPTER 4

"Right – that's quite enough work for one day," calls Miss Balogun. "You can all put your science books back in your drawers and then look this way." She pauses dramatically. "It's finally time for the big reveal!"

Tally shoves her book in her drawer and grins excitedly at Layla. Miss Balogun has been dropping not-so-subtle hints all week about having some exciting news, and they know exactly what it is that she's going to talk about. Tally has been waiting for this moment *all year*. There are lots of challenges about being in year six, but this, *this* is going to make up for all the difficulties and tough times.

Miss Balogun waits until everyone is quiet and then gives the class a big smile. "Now as you all know, we've got some hard work ahead of us between now and the year six tests."

Everyone groans.

"My brother said that they're a nightmare," shouts one of the girls. "He said that the questions are super difficult and make kids cry."

Miss Balogun takes a step forward and shakes her head. "They're really nothing to feel anxious about," she assures them. "You just have to do your best – I've been telling you that all year."

Tally isn't convinced. Miss Balogun *has* been telling them that since September, but the way her lips press tightly together whenever the subject of the year six tests comes up makes Tally think that Miss Balogun isn't entirely telling the truth when she says that they shouldn't be worried. And it's all very well saying that they just have to do their best, but what if your best isn't good enough? What happens then?

"Anyway, we're not talking about the tests right now." Miss Balogun leans back on her desk and raises one eyebrow. "What we're talking about is what happens *after* the tests. And that thing is, of course…"

She pauses again, really drawing out the moment. Tally leans forward in her seat.

"…The year six summer production!"

Everyone cheers, and there are even a few whoops

from the back of the class. Miss Balogun gives them a moment and then leans across her desk to press a key on her computer. The whiteboard behind her springs into life, and there on the screen, in full multicoloured glory, is the title page of the script.

"This year we're going to be putting on a performance of "*Little Red – The Untold Tale*," she announces. "And I am very excited about this one!"

"So we're just doing a fairy story?" asks Luke, sounding disappointed. "Like, for *babies*? Last year they did *Bugsy Malone*."

There is a rumbling sound as the class all start muttering amongst themselves.

"It's not *just* a fairy story," Miss Balogun tells them, pushing herself off the desk. "In fact, there's no such thing as 'just a fairy story'. If you look at them properly, fairy tales are dark, sinister fables created to teach children about the world – and if you ever read some of the older versions, then I guarantee you won't think that they're for babies."

She starts walking around the room, putting a piece of scrap paper on everyone's desk.

"*Little Red – The Untold Tale* has a twist. What if the wolf isn't an evil, granny-eating beast, but instead is constantly in the wrong place at the wrong time and unfairly getting the blame when things go badly? What if he's just trying to find a place to be safe? And what if Granny isn't a sweet old lady, but instead is a wolf-hunter, determined to rid the world of these troublesome creatures who don't fit in?"

"Did you know that the world record for the largest number of people howling simultaneously was achieved in 2017 in Canada, when eight hundred and three people all howled like wolves at the exact same time?" announces Miles.

Miss Balogun grins at him. "I did not know that, Miles. Did you by any chance take another *Guinness Book of Records* out of the library this week?"

Miles nods seriously, and Miss Balogun keeps moving around the room.

"What if Little Red doesn't really want to take her grandmother a basket of food because her granny is terrifying and unfriendly? And what if she ends up having to fight to protect the wolf from the people who don't understand him?"

She turns and looks at them all. "We're going to put on a production that will make everyone look at the story of Little Red Riding Hood in a whole new way. So, what I want you to do now is to write down the kind of role that you're interested in going for and put it on my desk. I'll start thinking about our cast list over the next few weeks. You can specify if you'd like a main role, in which case you need to be happy to learn a lot of lines and also to do some singing."

Tally sinks back in her seat and smiles to herself. Acting is absolutely her thing, and it's the one thing that she knows she is excellent at. She was born to play the lead in the summer production, and she knows that the role of Little Red is perfect. Tally would never let an animal be treated badly or unfairly, even by a granny.

"Or you can choose a minor role," continues the teacher, heading back to her desk. "Perhaps something with fewer lines. Or you can be in the chorus and do the singing. Last, but definitely not least, you can request a position as part of our technical crew who will be in charge of the all-important lights and sound."

Everyone grabs their piece of paper and starts to write. It takes Tally only seconds to record her choice and then she stands up and puts her piece of paper on Miss Balogun's desk.

Tally Olivia Adams – Little Red.

"I put down for a minor role," Layla tells her. "What about you?"

"Oh, I asked for a main part," Tally replies, trying to sound casual.

Layla beams at her. "You'd be a brilliant Little Red!" she says. "You're the best one at acting in the whole class, Tally!"

The warm feeling starts in Tally's stomach and spreads outward, making her cheeks glow. "Do you think so?" she asks.

Layla nods. "One hundred per cent. You're going to be Little Red and we're going to have so much fun rehearsing and it's all going to be amazing!"

In the distance, doors start to slam as the school day ends, and children erupt from their classrooms. Miss Balogun reminds them all about the homework due in tomorrow and then asks everyone to collect their things and line up at the door.

But Tally doesn't move for a moment, even though the room around her is filled with noise and activity. She sits very still and lets her mind wander to what it's going to be like when she gets the part; to how it's going to feel to be the most popular kid in year six because the person who plays the lead role in the summer production is *always* the most popular. She knows that Layla believes in her – that's what a best friend does – but she also knows that as far as the rest of year six are concerned, she's not exactly the best. She's going to show everyone what she can do, and it's going to feel amazing to be her for once. Everything is finally going to start working out – she just *knows* it.

CHAPTER 5

"Girls, I need you to set the table for supper, please!"

Mum's voice floats through from the room next door. It used to be the dining room, but once she started painting full-time, it was decided that they could eat in the kitchen and that the dining room could be turned into her art studio. Well, Mum and Dad decided. They didn't ask Tally what she thought of their plan, but if they had she'd have told them that it was a terrible idea. The dining room looks out on to the garden and it's peaceful. It's a nice, relaxing place to eat, unlike the kitchen with all the food smells and constant noise.

"I'm busy," mumbles Nell, not looking up from her phone. "You can do it."

Tally stares at her sister through the eyes of the tiger mask that Dad brought home for her from his last work trip away. She's got several masks, but even though she hasn't had this one long, it's quickly become her favourite. Whenever she wears it, she feels safe.

"You're not busy," she points out. "You're just messing about on your phone. How is that any busier than me listening to music?"

Nell sighs. "I'm working," she huffs, rolling her eyes. "For your information, I'm asking Rosa about the homework assignment that we got today, so be a good little girl and set the table. And it's not music, it's Taylor Swift, and if I have to listen to that terrible song one more time, I'm going to go mad."

Tally isn't sure if it's the eye-roll, the *good little girl* comment or the rude comment about Taylor's music, but she's aware that her good mood has completely disappeared.

"No."

She reaches for the iPad and turns up the volume.

Nell glances up and scowls at her. "Yes. I've got stuff to do and you don't. Just do what Mum wants, OK?"

Taylor Swift's voice fills the room as the iPad is increased to maximum volume.

Tally's voice, on the other hand, is very, very quiet. "You can't tell me what to do."

She thinks that she's maybe a little bit like an iceberg. Nell can only see the tiniest tip of how she's feeling, and maybe it doesn't look like much, but she should watch out because beneath the surface there is a whole lot more going on.

"Well, I can actually." Nell sounds cold but she's not a match for Tally's icy depths. "I'm fourteen years old and you're only ten, so you have to do as I say. And I say to stop being difficult and set the table."

Tally always thought that fire melted ice, but she must be wrong because the intense burning sensation in her head only makes the block of ice in her chest feel even bigger. She launches off the sofa and flings herself at Nell, grabbing her phone and throwing it as hard as she can across the room.

"I am *not* difficult!" she screams. "Take that back!"

"Get *off* me!" yelps Nell, struggling to keep Tally's hands away from her face. "Mum!"

She tries to shake Tally off, but Tally reaches out and grips hold of whatever she can, determined not to let go. Footsteps pound down the hallway and then Mum bursts into the room.

"Girls! What on earth is going on?"

"Get her off me!" screeches Nell. "She's gone crazy!"

"Don't call me that word!" snarls Tally, tightening her grip, like a tiger grasping on to an antelope.

Mum strides across the living room and yanks Tally backwards. Unfortunately, Tally is not prepared for this movement, and the scream of pain from Nell as a chunk of her hair is pulled away in her sister's hand is so loud that it makes Tally's ears hurt.

"What was that all about?" asks Mum, reaching out for Nell. "Are you all right?"

"No! I am not all right!" howls Nell, clutching her head. "She ripped out my *hair*, Mum! You've got to do something about her – she's completely wild. It's not normal."

"I'm not all right either," murmurs Tally. "If anyone is interested."

Mum turns off the iPad and turns to face her. "No, Tally. I'm afraid that I'm *not* particularly interested in how you're feeling right now. We told you after the last time you hurt your sister that this has to stop, and yet here we are again. Now take off that mask and look at me properly."

"She attacked me," sniffs Nell. "I'm not safe in my own home."

Mum breathes out a very long, slow breath. "There's no need to bring the full dramatics, thank you, Nell. What

45

Tally did was wrong, and she's going to make it better."

Tally steps closer to Mum, the tiger mask still firmly on her head.

"Aren't you going to ask me what she did to deserve it? You always say that there are two sides to every story, and you haven't even heard mine yet."

Mum doesn't speak for a moment and instead stares at the window, almost as if she'd rather be outside in the rain than in the room with them. Then she gives herself a little shake and looks at Tally.

"I'm going to ask you one question, Tally, and I want you to tell me the truth. Did Nell hurt you first?"

Tally nods enthusiastically. "Yes! She totally did!"

Nell stands up and glowers at her sister. "That's a lie and you know it. I didn't touch you. I'd never hit you or treat you the way that you treat me."

Mum stares at her youngest daughter. "Is that true?"

Tally scowls at Nell. "She *did* hurt me first. She said really unkind things and she hurt my feelings."

"I asked her to set the table because I was doing homework," Nell informs Mum.

"Liar! You *told* me," retorts Tally. "You didn't *ask* me."

Mum's shoulders slump. "Oh, *Tally*," she says quietly. "Go to your room, please. And while you're sitting up there on your own, I want you to think about what you've done wrong and how this whole thing could have been avoided."

Nell gives Tally a death stare behind Mum's back. It's OK for her. Nell was born with all the luck in the world, and some days Tally is convinced that this is part of the problem. Mum always says that Nell was born under a lucky star, which makes Tally suspect that it must have been particularly cloudy on the night of her birth. Then again, Nell is so horrible that it wouldn't surprise Tally if she'd just taken more than her share and there was no luck left by the time Tally was born.

Mum gestures towards the doorway. "Go on. And when you come down for supper I expect you to apologize to your sister."

Tally doesn't care. They can't make her say sorry, and she'd rather be in her bedroom listening to Taylor Swift than down here with her uncaring family. The tiger slinks towards the door, keen to retreat to its den. Nell can get as much attention and sympathy from Mum as she wants – what she's failing to understand is that Tally can't possibly set the kitchen table if she's been sent to her room, and so Nell is going to have to do it after all. Which is completely fair considering that this was all her fault in the first place.

Factfile homework

Name of Person

~~Jennifer Adams~~

Taylor Swift

Most important thing about them

~~She is my mum. She's also an artist but that's not as imortant as being my mum. I know this because she's always telling me.~~

Her incredible music.

What you admire about them

~~She puts up with me even when I'm "being hard work". She says that she still loves me even when I've hurt her or punched a hole in the wall or broken something special.~~

Taylor never gives up and she's always there for her fans, no matter what.

What you dislike about them

~~She sends me to my room when things have gone wrong~~
~~and it doesn't help me at all. I want to be sat down and~~
~~treated like a human being, not sent away.~~ That makes
me feel like I'm just a situation that people don't want to
deal with. ~~Sometimes I need help with my feelings~~ but they
send me off to deal with them alone. ~~And that is scary.~~

I don't dislike anything about Taylor Swift. The end.

What you wish you could tell them

~~I'm sorry that I get so angry and always make everything~~
~~nice turn bad. I used to convince myself that everyone~~
~~else was just the same, but when I went to Layla's house~~
~~there were no holes in the wall or broken anything. I'm~~
~~sorry you got so unlucky with me.~~

I am your biggest fan and I will always be there for you,
just like I know you're there for me.

CHAPTER 6

"*I don't see why I had to come,*" whines Tally as they get out of the car. It's not the first time that she's uttered these words in the past twenty minutes, and she hears Dad mutter something under his breath.

"Because it's *your* parents' evening," Mum tells her again. "And it's important that you're here to listen to what Miss Balogun has to say about how you're getting on."

Tally slams the car door. "She doesn't even *know me*. I bet she hasn't got a clue about how I'm getting on."

They walk towards the main school entrance, Tally lagging behind. The truth is that she can't bear the thought of people talking about her when she isn't there, and if Mum and Dad had left her at home with Nell then she'd have been *really* miserable. It's just that the idea of

50

sitting in the classroom and being forced to listen to Miss Balogun talk about her is also quite awful.

The door to the year six room is open as they walk up the stairs and Miss Balogun waves them inside.

"I'm actually running on time for a change!" she laughs.

Mum and Dad laugh too, and Tally resists the urge to groan. Nobody has said anything even vaguely amusing, but adults always do this, and as far as Tally is concerned it's a complete waste of energy. People should keep their laughs for things that are genuinely funny, not go around wasting them on stupid comments that don't mean anything.

"Have a seat," says Miss Balogun, gesturing towards the row of chairs that are facing her desk. Dad squeezes himself onto the furthest one, his knees almost touching his forehead, and Tally swallows a giggle. Now *that* is something that is *actually* funny.

"So, Tally." Miss Balogun waits until they're all sitting down and then steeples her fingers together under her chin and gazes at her pupil. "How do *you* think year six is going so far?"

Tally stares back at her. She thought the entire point of parents' evening was for *Miss Balogun* to tell *them* how she was doing. If it's going to be up to her to do the talking then she could have done that back at home and not have to be dragged away from watching TV. And what's she meant to say? Does Miss Balogun want her to talk about how sad she feels at lunchtimes when nobody will play her games? Or maybe to tell Mum and Dad about how sometimes, when she's supposed to be working, it feels like a hive of bees has taken up residence in her head and all she can hear is a constant buzzing so that when the lesson is over, her writing looks like a scrawled mess of words? Or perhaps how when Miss Balogun is giving a long talk to the class about whatever it is they're supposed to be learning, she feels bored and freaked out at the same time, which is not a good feeling because you'd have thought one of those things would cancel out the other and they aren't supposed to exist together.

She plays it safe and shrugs. Nobody can get upset about a shrug.

Miss Balogun smiles. "Well, I can tell you that you're doing just fine in year six, Tally." She looks at Tally's parents and beams. "She's a delightful girl and a pleasure to have in the class."

There's a moment of pause and then Mum shifts in her seat.

"That's wonderful to hear – really, it is." She glances at

Dad. "We were just wondering if you'd seen any change in Tally over the past few months? If maybe she needed a little more support with her behaviour in the classroom?"

Miss Balogun laughs. "Behaviour?" She tilts her head on one side and looks at Mum. "Tally is a model pupil, Mrs Adams. She hasn't been given a yellow sanction card, let alone a red card. That's right, isn't it, Tally?"

Tally nods. Plenty of kids have been given yellow and red cards over the year and had to miss out on Friday afternoon Golden Time activities, but not Tally. She actually hates Golden Time – the classroom is hot and noisy, and everyone seems to know exactly what they're supposed to be doing except her. She'd really like to spend it sitting in the book corner drawing pictures of her riding on Peaches, but Miles always sits there with his *Guinness Book of World Records*, and everyone would definitely tease her if she sat with him. Even so, she would never do anything that would make Miss Balogun give her a sanction card. She has to be good at school – that's a rule.

"That's not to say that she doesn't have any targets, though," continues the teacher. Tally scuffs her feet on the floor. Of *course* she has targets. It's never enough to just say nice things about a person or their work – there always has to be something wrong.

"I'm wondering if we could have a quick chat with you in private?" asks Mum, reaching for Dad's knee and giving it a quick squeeze.

Miss Balogun frowns slightly but then nods. "Of course. Tally – why don't you wait outside in the corridor? There are some books out there."

Tally stands up and walks out of the room, not looking at her parents. She doesn't want anyone to see how she's feeling right now. All that fuss about making her come with them when they planned on kicking her out of the room anyway? She can't show how upset she is, not when Miss Balogun would see, but she also can't keep it bottled up for ever, so they'd better not take too long in there.

She pulls the door almost closed behind her and then stands right next to it, listening to their voices. It's not hard to hear them – she's always had exceptionally good hearing, which at times like this is very useful indeed.

"... always been challenging at home, but there's been a real shift in the past few months." Mum's voice floats through the crack in the doorway.

"She can be quite aggressive at times, and she's becoming increasingly, well – the only word for it is *violent*, particularly towards her sister." It's Dad speaking now, and Tally leans closer to the door. "She gets angry every time we ask her to do anything. We just wondered if you'd noticed anything at school?"

Tally clenches her fists tightly and squeezes her eyes closed. How dare they say that to her teacher? That's *home* stuff – it's got nothing to do with school. And it's not like she just attacks Nell, is it? Nell always does something to her first, but nobody's talking about *that* or how unlucky she is to have such a horrible big sister.

Miss Balogun sounds puzzled. "I really haven't. I mean, she's quite a shy, quiet girl, and I know she doesn't like taking risks in her learning, but she's where she's supposed to be right now in terms of her levels. I'd like to see her improving her confidence and self-esteem before year seven, but we're working on that."

Dad makes a strange noise with his throat. "Shy? Quiet? Are we talking about the same child here?"

I told you that she doesn't know me. Tally clamps her lips shut so that the words don't escape. They wouldn't be fair anyway. She *is* quiet when she's in class because nobody can tease you or mock you for saying stuff if you just *don't*. She's learnt that the hard way. And Miss Balogun has always been kind to her – it's not her fault that school is such a lot.

"We're just worried about her," says Mum in a rush, and Tally can picture her face looking all screwed up. "I've been doing some research and I've been wondering about autism."

Outside the door, Tally opens her eyes.

This is new.

"I don't think you need to worry about that," says Miss Balogun, in the same soothing voice she uses when someone's upset because they've got their maths wrong. "I have some experience of teaching autistic children, and Tally isn't displaying any of the characteristics that they do. She makes excellent eye contact and, while she does seem to be getting into a few more altercations with the other children in the playground at the moment, she does have a few friends. And I haven't seen any of the typical autism behaviours in her – she doesn't have any obsessions, for example."

She must be talking about Miles. He always looks away if he needs to talk to someone, and he doesn't have any friends. Plus, he's totally hooked on his world records books, which must be what Miss Balogun means by *obsessions*.

"What about the pencil cases?" points out Mum. "She's pretty obsessive about them."

Miss Balogun laughs. "That's very normal for a year six girl."

"Or the constant listening to Taylor Swift? The way she talks about her, you'd think they were best friends. And if she gets interrupted while she's listening to her music then all hell breaks loose."

"Again – it's probably just a fad."

"It's not really what I'd call a fad, though," says Mum. "More of a complete infatuation. And she's just so different to her sister."

Miss Balogun makes a humming noise. "Well, perhaps I can see that she is a *little* different to the other kids, but we really aren't seeing anything in school that is cause for concern. And children *are* all different – that's the wonderful thing about teaching them!"

"So it's a home issue, then?" says Dad, sounding relieved. "She's just a bit *different*."

Tally shifts from one foot to the other.

"That would be my feeling," says Miss Balogun. "I'll certainly keep an eye on her, and if the situation changes in school then we can put some additional help in place. But as it stands, she's doing fine. We've obviously got a challenging term ahead of us, but after that we'll be focused on the summer production, which should be a lot of fun!"

"Yes, Tally's excited about that." Mum's voice sounds as flat as a pancake.

"Well, considering everything you've told me, I think I might just reconsider the part I'm going to give her," confides Miss Balogun. "I think I have the perfect role to help her thrive and gain a little more confidence as well as developing her team-working skills."

Tally steps away from the door and slumps down on to a comfy chair, ignoring the pile of books beside her. She should be feeling happy that she's got the role of Little Red – Miss Balogun just basically confirmed it – but as usual Mum and Dad have taken all the happiness away.

The sound of voices wafts up the staircase, and Tally watches as a man and a boy appear around the corner.

"I don't see why I had to come," moans the man.

"The teacher wanted to see you," says the boy.

The man huffs out a long breath. "Yeah, well – I never had to do this before."

"That's because Mum always—" Luke breaks off as he sees Tally sitting outside the classroom door. They stare at each other for a long moment and then Tally looks away.

She's fairly sure that Luke won't call her horrible names with his dad standing right next to him, but she can't be entirely sure.

"Are you ready to go home?" Suddenly Mum is standing in front of her, reaching out to pull her up. Tally ignores her and grabs the car keys that are dangling from her hand before storming down the stairs ahead of her parents.

"Wait up!" calls Dad as she races towards the car. "Tally!"

But Tally can't hear him. All she can hear is the sound of their voices as they told all those lies, lies, lies about her. She isn't *aggressive* or *angry* or *violent*. She isn't *quiet* or *shy* either. Those aren't the right words at all, and she might not know what the right words *are*, but she can feel them inside her, trying to push their way out of her body. It feels like they might suffocate her if she can't find her voice.

Scraaaatch.

The high-pitched noise releases a tiny bit of pressure in her chest and she takes a deeper breath, filling her lungs with air. *She's different to her sister.*

Raaassssp.

Her teeth squeak and she winces, but she doesn't stop because the sound is focusing her attention on the important things. *She's different to the other kids.*

Scrrrrrrape.

Her arm moves in a long sweep. That's the word she was looking for. The word that describes who she is. *She's just a bit different.*

The keys judder in her hand and then fall to the floor as Dad takes hold of her arm.

His voice is barely a whisper, which is far more terrifying than a shout. "What have you *done*?"

Tally blinks and contemplates the scene before her. The deep gouge runs all the way along the side of Mum's new car like a jagged wound that needs stitches.

"Oh, my…" Beside her, Mum clasps her hand to her mouth. "*Why*, Tally? Why did you do such a terrible thing?"

Tally feels tears dripping down her face, which is surprising because she didn't even know that she was crying.

"You were right," murmurs Dad. "We do need to get some help. We need to fix this."

Mum nods. "We can't carry on this way."

Tally doesn't know what this means, but she does know one thing.

Her parents think that she's different and needs fixing.

Which means she must be broken.

A TALE OF TWO TALLY'S

SCHOOL TALLY
Careful thinker
Silent watcher
Rule maker
School helper
If you looked through our classroom door, then you
probably wouldn't even notice me.

HOME TALLY
Bad loser
Fast talker
Law breaker
Chaos creator

What happens at home is for home, and what happens at
school is for school. Two different places where I am two
different people, and I have worked so hard to make sure
that Home Tally doesn't go to school.

With every scratch of the keys against the car, I could
feel the fire escaping my body a little more. But then
they were yelling at me and I was screaming to try and
stop myself thinking, or doing anything else bad.

I was screaming for someone to make all of this go away.
I was screaming for help.
Even if they couldn't hear me.

CHAPTER 7

It would be nice to say that the next few weeks pass by in a blur, but unfortunately for Tally the opposite is true. The hours at school drag on and on in a relentless cycle of practice tests and extra maths, and Miss Balogun constantly telling them that they just have to do their best and then making them do yet *another* reading comprehension. Tally tries her hardest, but the air in the classroom seems to get heavier every day, and sometimes she thinks that it's impossible to do anything except survive, which is tricky when every time she *does* do anything, someone gets upset with her.

It's not like any of it is even her fault. Like last week, when Miss Balogun told them all to work in groups to recreate the solar system using polystyrene balls. Tally's group got really angry when she insisted on including

Pluto, because they all said that it wasn't a planet any more. And even though she tried to tell them that it isn't fair to kick Pluto out of the solar system because you can't take something like that away just because you've decided to change the rules, they said that she was spoiling the model. And then Miss Balogun told them all off for a) not working well as a group and b) not listening to the names of the planets in the solar system. So nobody except Layla would talk to her for the rest of the week.

Home isn't much better. Mum and Dad spend hours huddled together in Mum's studio, hunched over her laptop and murmuring in whispers that they don't want Tally to hear. They're talking about her, she knows it. And the knowing makes her tummy feel like it's filled with tiny stones and her head feel like it's been stuffed with the same polystyrene balls that their disastrous solar system was made from.

Their words ooze through the crack in the door and slither their way into Tally's ears where they slide and squirm and burrow into her brain like the parasitic worms she saw on a nature documentary a few weeks ago.

Meltdowns.

Demand Avoidance.

Autistic Spectrum Disorder.

Different. Different. Different.

So it is something of a relief when Miss Balogun gets the class together in the hall at the end of a sunny Friday afternoon and tells them that she's ready to share the cast list for the summer production. Tally is certainly ready for some good news for a change.

"I wonder which role I'm going to get," says Layla as they sit down on the benches that are arranged in a large square. "I hope I'm one of the squirrels! They only have a few lines, but they've got a great song!"

Tally doesn't answer. On the outside she looks calm and relaxed, like none of this really matters to her. On the inside, her heart is pounding as she rehearses what she's going to say when Miss Balogun announces her for the lead role. It's important that she gets it right because this is where everything is going to change. The other kids in year six are all finally going to see what she can do, and Mum and Dad will stop having their secret conversations – because if she's good enough to be the star of the performance, then nobody will think that she needs fixing.

And Tally cannot wait to actually feel *good enough*, just for once.

"OK, year six! Are you ready?" asks Miss Balogun,

stepping inside the square. "I've spent a lot of time considering this and I hope you're all going to be happy! I've tried to give you all a role that will use your wonderful strengths, and even if it may challenge you a little, I think you're going to all excel at the part you've been given."

She smiles and looks right at Tally.

Layla squeals quietly and nudges Tally with her elbow.

"You're so going to be Little Red!"

Tally grins back. She hasn't told anyone that she overheard Miss Balogun tell her parents that she was being given a role where she could *thrive* and *gain in confidence* because she's been working hard to forget everything about that evening. But now the time is here and she's ready.

It's her moment, and for the first time in a while, she's feeling like she's due some luck.

"So, first, the part of the wolf is going to Luke!"

Everyone swivels on the benches to stare at Luke, who isn't looking entirely thrilled.

Tally frowns. Luke is not a good choice for the part of the misunderstood wolf. He's unkind and rude and he calls her mean names – what is there to misunderstand about that?

"Next, we're going to have Ameet as the woodcutter!"

Tally supposes that this was a slightly better casting decision on Miss Balogun's part. The woodcutter is the comedian of the performance, and Ameet can be quite funny.

Miss Balogun clears her throat. "I'm very happy to tell you all that the role of Little Red is going to be played by ..."

Tally arranges her face into the smile she's been working on at home. It's meant to show that she is happy and surprised and excited and also a bit amazed, which is quite a lot to ask of a smile, but she's pretty sure that she's got it nailed.

"... Carrie!"

The hall erupts in an explosion of applause and whooping. On the opposite bench, Carrie's cheeks glow bright red and the smile on her face doesn't look like she's even bothered to practise it.

"You're going to be incredible!" screeches Ayesha.

"Well done, Carrie!" yells someone else. "You'll be a perfect Little Red."

"Thanks," stutters Carrie. "I didn't even put down for a main part."

Miss Balogun raises her hand for quiet. "We've all heard you sing though, Carrie! You're the perfect choice for the part, and I just know that you're going to do a marvellous job."

"You'd have been a much better choice, Tally," whispers Layla, faithfully. "Carrie gets scared if she's asked to answer a question in class."

"But Miss Balogun wants someone who can perform the solo, and Carrie *can* sing," adds Lucy, on her other side.

But I can sing.

The words stay deep inside Tally's head.

I can sing. Why doesn't anybody know that?

Am I actually invisible?

Miss Balogun continues to allocate the parts and Tally sits motionless, barely listening as she tries to figure out how everything has gone so badly. Little Red was *her* part. At least she thought it was.

"And finally, and possibly most importantly, we have our technical crew." Miss Balogun folds up her piece of paper and nods. "Without calm, steady hands to provide us with our lights and sound, there would be no production. And this year, our fabulous tech crew is going to be Miles and Tally!"

She claps her hands, and everyone dutifully joins in, but there's no whooping and cheering like there was for Carrie.

"Brilliant!" Miles sounds pleased. "I've already taken a look at the light board and I think, with a bit of tweaking of the electronics, we can make it really spectacular!"

"There will be no tweaking of any electronics," Miss Balogun tells him sternly, although her eyes are twinkling. "Do you understand me, Miles?"

"No. I'm not doing that." Tally's voice is quiet, but everybody hears her and a few people gasp. "I want to be Little Red. I'll be better at it than Carrie will. She gets scared if she has to answer a question in class."

Across the room, Carrie stares at the ground, looking like she wants to disappear.

"Oh, Taaally," groans Ayesha.

"Don't make a fuss about it," hisses Lucy.

Miss Balogun looks at Tally for a long moment and then turns away.

"Let's put the benches back and then head up to class to get ready for home time," Miss Balogun announces.

"You shouldn't have said that about Carrie," whispers Layla as everyone gets up. "You hurt her feelings."

Tally stares at her. "You said it first," she points out.

"But it's totally different. I said it quietly so that Carrie wouldn't hear." Layla sighs. "I was trying to make you feel better."

Tally does not feel better. If anything, she feels worse.

"I didn't get the part that I wanted either," confides Layla as they walk out of the hall. "I'm Villager Number Five, which doesn't sound that good."

Tally doesn't reply. She doesn't want her best friend to tell her about her boring part. She wants her to rage for her, to fight for her, to storm up to Miss Balogun and tell her that she's made a massive mistake. It's what Tally would do for Layla if she'd been treated so unfairly.

Besides, she's got more important things to think about than rubbish Villager Number Five. Once again, everything has gone wrong for her, but there's a tiny voice in her head that won't stop niggling away, and the things it's suggesting are making it impossible to hear anything else.

What if she is doomed to constantly have bad luck?

What if, no matter what she does, nobody ever gives her a chance?

What if she *is* actually different?

CHAPTER 8

"It's going to be all right," says Mum, stroking Tally's head.

Tally doesn't see how this can possibly be true, but it's nice snuggling up to Mum like a little kitten and letting her try to make it better.

"Can I have a snack?"

Nell and the biscuit tin appear in the doorway. It takes a second for her to notice Tally's tear-streaked face. "What's the big drama now, then?"

"*Nell.*" Mum's voice holds a warning. "Tally's had a bit of a day at school and she needs us all to be kind."

Tally sits up straight.

"I've not had a *bit* of a day," she tells Mum. "I've had a *lot* of a day. That's the problem."

Mum nods as if she understands. "We all have days like that sometimes. The important thing is to move on and remember that tomorrow is a new day: a fresh start."

Tally slumps back down on to the sofa. Mum is doing her best, but it isn't helping. Tomorrow isn't the problem. Tomorrow is Saturday, and she can spend all day in bed if she wants to. It's Monday that's the issue.

"So, what's happened?" asks Nell, pulling the lid off the biscuit tin and becoming immediately distracted. "Did you buy more chocolate fingers?"

Mum shakes her head. "Tally is a bit—" She breaks off when Tally turns to glare at her and starts again. "—a *lot* upset. She's had a tough day at school, although she apparently doesn't want to talk about it. And no – I haven't been shopping yet."

"Oh." Nell turns to go. "I thought something bad had happened."

"It *is* bad!" Tally leaps up and starts pacing the room. "And I'm never going back to school ever again."

Nell walks across to Tally and offers her the biscuit tin. "Have a biscuit. Biscuits make everything better."

"They do," agrees Tally, taking a plain digestive. She isn't entirely sure what is going on, because Nell is never usually this nice to her, but she thinks she likes it.

"I'm going to make a start on supper, so you can only have one biscuit each," says Mum, getting off the sofa.

"I'm sorry that today has been tricky, Tally – but at least it's the weekend now. And you know where I am if you do want to chat about what happened."

She walks out of the room and Nell and Tally look at each other. It's been a while since they had a conversation where one of them wasn't screaming at the other, and they both seem a little unsure about what they should be doing.

"So what's the problem?" asks Nell, reaching for another biscuit.

"There's no point in telling *you*," mumbles Tally through a mouthful of crumbs. "You can't help me."

"Whatever." Nell puts the lid on the tin, which is a little unfair when she's had two biscuits and Tally has only had one, but Tally doesn't think she can handle yet another crisis today so she lets it go. Nell flops down into an armchair, pulls out her phone and starts swiping the screen, and Tally suddenly finds the words flowing from her mouth.

"Everything keeps going wrong for me, and I just wanted one thing to be right, that's all. I wanted people to think that I was the *good one* for a change," She sniffs. "It's probably stupid."

"I thought you didn't want to talk about it?" Nell

doesn't look up from her phone. "And I also thought that you don't care about what other people think? You say it often enough."

Tally shrugs. Not caring is harder than she thought it would be.

"It'd just be nice for something to work out," she tells Nell, leaning against the wall. "Instead of me always being so totally unlucky."

Nell sighs and glances up.

"Why are you always so sorry for yourself?" she asks, and Tally remembers that her sister is actually a complete pain in the neck. "Do something about it, then, if it matters that much to you."

Tally frowns. "What do you mean? What am I supposed to do?"

Nell's phone beeps and she starts typing out a message. "I don't know, do I? Just stop feeling like everyone's out to get you just because you didn't get your own way. *Do* something about it and sort your own problems instead of constantly moaning like a baby." Nell groans. "You're so annoying sometimes."

Tally pushes herself off the wall and pulls a face at Nell, who doesn't notice because she only has eyes for her phone these days.

"I really hate you," Tally whispers. On another day the hurt, upset feeling that is swirling through her would rage out through her hands and feet and mouth like a volcano, and Nell would be sorry that she'd said something so unkind. Today though, Tally hasn't got enough energy. She isn't a volcano today. Instead, she's the ground after an earthquake, all cracked and shaken. Nell's cruel words are just the aftershock to the main event of school and the summer production casting.

Tally leaves the room, and her diabolical sister, and walks slowly upstairs. She never usually listens to anything that Nell has to say, but she *is* right about one thing. Tally has *got* to do something about her problems and quickly if she doesn't want everything to get completely out of her control. As far as she can see, she has three problems and she needs three solutions.

Problem one: she wants to play Little Red in the performance, but Miss Balogun has given the part to Carrie. She could tell Miss Balogun that she isn't prepared to be part of the tech crew and that she'll only be in the production if she can play Little Red, but that won't sort anything. There's no way that Miss Balogun will give her the part if she thinks that Tally is behaving badly. And Mum and Dad will just add her refusal to join in on to their long list of *Things Tally Has Done Wrong*.

Which leads her to problem two: Mum and Dad haven't stopped their muttered conversations, and Tally has overheard them using the word "autism" more than once now, as well as stuff like "need some help" and "can't go on like this", which makes Tally feel like she's *their* problem that needs to be solved. And that's just not true. If autism looks like Miles then there's absolutely no way that it applies to her too – she couldn't be more different to Miles if she tried (and she *does* try – she tries very hard).

But then there's problem three: people keep using the word *different* when they're talking about her. And different is very, very bad. In fact, it's the reason for problems one and two, and it's why they're trying to call her a word that she can't be when the only word they should be calling her is *Tally*.

Once she's inside her room, Tally sits down at her desk and stares at her reflection in the mirror. A tired face stares back at her, and she wonders how everyone else deals with it, day after day, when just trying to figure out life is so utterly exhausting.

She doesn't want to do the lights for the school production, but she *does* want to be part of the play. Acting makes her happy and it's the one time she feels kind of good about herself. Plus, she's been waiting for *years* to do the year six production. If she makes a fuss and says that she won't work with Miles, then there's a risk that she could lose any chance of being involved, and that would be terrible, even if nobody does think she's capable of doing anything except pressing some buttons and flicking some switches.

She's going to have to be cleverer than that. She's going to need a plan.

CHAPTER 9

Monday morning does not get off to a promising start.

"What does EP mean?" asks Tally, staring at the family calendar.

"Hmm?" Mum isn't listening. "Do you want cheese or ham in your sandwich today?"

Tally frowns. She always has cheese. She used to have ham until she saw a documentary on her iPad about pigs, and now the very thought of ham makes her feel squirmy inside.

"Why is it written under my name for next month?" She stares at the letters. She doesn't know what they stand for, but something is telling her that it isn't anything good.

"Why is *what* written *where*?" asks Mum, yanking open the fridge door. "We're out of cheese. It'll have to be ham."

Tally stamps her foot and Mum finally looks at her.

"Please not today, Tally. I've got a major meeting at the art gallery and Dad had to go in to work early, so I need you onboard this morning."

"I. Hate. Ham," hisses Tally through her teeth.

Mum starts buttering two slices of bread. "Fine. You can have a bread sandwich instead."

Tally watches as Mum places the two slices together and then cuts them into neat squares before putting them into Tally's lunchbox along with an apple, some raisins and a cereal bar.

"What is EP?" she repeats.

Maybe she's got it wrong. Perhaps it *is* something good? It could mean lots of things.

Exciting Prize.

Entertaining Person.

Then again it could be bad.

Eavesdropping Pest.

Exasperated Parent.

"I'm going to give you some grapes, too," says Mum. "Maybe you can make a grape sandwich at lunchtime? And we've got an appointment to see someone in a few weeks – just for a chat."

"Who?" Tally is instantly suspicious. "What about?"

Mum smiles at her, but while her mouth manages to

turn itself upwards, her eyes don't get the message. "It's nothing to worry about," she assures Tally. "We just want to get a bit of help for you, lovely girl."

Those are the words that her lying mouth says, anyway. The words that she actually means and the words that fling themselves deep into Tally's head are entirely the opposite.

It's *everything* to worry about.

"Are you seeing a doctor, then?" asks Nell, looking up from her bowl of cereal.

"Kind of," says Mum. "She's sort of like a doctor who helps figure out what's going on inside people's heads."

If someone told Tally at this exact moment that the world had stopped rotating then she would believe it. Everything seems to stand still while she contemplates what Mum has just said. She isn't sick and she doesn't need a doctor. And she absolutely does *not* want to meet anyone who can see what's going on inside her head, because when she imagines her thoughts, she pictures them a bit like a tangled, knotted-up piece of wool, and she likes it that way. The last thing she wants is someone pulling on the end and unravelling it all.

Unravelling her.

She can't let this happen.

The morning becomes worse when Nell can't find her homework book and gets all angry, and then Mum gets even angrier when it's eventually tracked down in Tally's room. Tally tells a red-faced Nell that maybe next time she won't call her an *annoying baby*, which makes Nell stomp downstairs so loudly that one of the picture frames fall off the wall.

The one with Tally cuddling a baby lamb at the petting zoo, obviously. Not the one of Nell with the alpacas. She's far too lucky to break one of her *own* pictures.

Then Tally's socks feel wrong, and Mum won't listen when Tally tries to tell her that she needs a different pair. Tally has to hide under the duvet and refuse to come out until Mum finds her a pair that doesn't feel so scratchy.

By the time they reach the school gates, the playground is empty.

Mum hands Tally her lunchbox.

"I'll see you later," she tells her, leaning down to give her a kiss. "You'd better hurry – you're quite late."

Tally lurches away, moving her head rapidly from side to side to check that nobody is watching. She can't remember when Mum trying to kiss her or hug her in public became the worst thing ever, but there's no *way* she can cope with the thought of anyone seeing anything so humiliating. It's bad enough when Mum starts laughing in that loud way that she has. Tally has tried to tell her to stop, but the first few times it just made her laugh even more, and then it made her face crumple up like she was going to cry. Both of these things left Tally feeling all empty inside, like a leaky bucket.

"Oh, Tally," sighs Mum. "Try to have a good day."

Tally walks across the playground, not turning to wave at Mum when she reaches the entrance. She's sick and tired of hearing those words. If anyone ever wrote the story of her life then they'd probably call it *Oh, Tally*, because that's all anyone ever seems to say to her these days.

Her feet slow down as she trudges up the stairs. She's in no rush to get into the classroom. She knows exactly what she's going to find – everyone eagerly talking about the production and Carrie and the songs and her wonderful voice, and she needs some time to put on her *I don't care* face.

She hangs her coat on her peg in the cloakroom and then sits down on the bench that runs beneath it. She can't stay out here for long, but she can at least delay her entrance to the classroom by a few minutes. The cloakroom is quiet, so when she hears the noise it startles her enough to make her leap to her feet. The high-pitched keening sounds like an injured animal, and her heart starts to race. Spinning round, she stares hard at the corner of the cloakroom where a pile of coats is lying on the bench, wondering if maybe a badger or a fox or perhaps a cat has snuck inside to keep safe. She really hopes it isn't a badger. Tally loves all animals, but some of them are a bit less cute and cuddly than others.

She takes a careful step forward, and the pile of coats shifts and rearranges itself into something recognizable. Tally releases the breath that she didn't know she was holding.

"Oh. It's only you."

The thing making the noise is the opposite of cute and cuddly, and Tally would rather confront one hundred badgers than one of him.

The noise stops abruptly, and Luke's face emerges from the coats. It's wet, and if Tally didn't know him better then she'd think he'd been crying.

"Get lost, weirdo," he snarls. "Shouldn't you be somewhere playing imaginary horse games like a three-year-old?"

Tally glowers at him. "Shut up," she snaps back. "I'm not the one hiding."

He straightens up and narrows his eyes at her. "Oh

yeah? Cos you don't exactly look like you're in a hurry to get into class."

"I'm telling Miss Balogun that you're out here," Tally retorts, turning and walking towards the year six door. She might not want to go in there, but it's got to be better than staying anywhere that awful Luke is.

"Not if I get there first." He barges past her and flings open the door. "Sorry I'm late, Miss Balogun! My gran needed someone to get her some bread and there was nobody else to do it."

Tally follows him inside. There's no way Miss Balogun is going to believe that. Everyone knows that Luke is vile and doesn't care about anyone except himself. Not even his gran.

Miss Balogun turns away from the whiteboard and looks at Luke with a strange expression on her face. Tally slips into her seat and waits for the explosion. Miss Balogun is a pretty calm teacher, but the one thing she can't stand is lying.

"That was very kind of you, Luke," she says, and Tally shakes her head, wondering if she's heard correctly. "Your gran is a very lucky lady to have such a considerate grandson."

Luke smiles and walks to the back of the room, giving

Ameet a high-five as he passes. Miss Balogun starts to hand out the English books, and Tally pulls out her newest pencil case, the sequin one that she convinced Mum to buy for her at the weekend.

"I love that!" exclaims Layla, reaching out to touch the sequins. "Where did you get it?"

But Tally doesn't hear her. Instead, her brain is whirring as she thinks about what just happened and how Luke, the worst boy in the school, managed to convince an actual adult that he is *good* just by telling her what she wanted to hear.

Miss Balogun reaches Tally's desk and puts her English book down.

"Have you had any more thoughts about being part of the technical crew?" she asks Tally quietly, leaning forward. "I know that you asked for a bigger part, but I really think you'll do a fantastic job with the lights, and you and Miles will make a great team. I was a little disappointed with your reaction last week."

From the corner of her eye, Tally sees Layla anxiously looking at her. Layla knows her better than anyone else at school, and she's the only person who has ever seen what Tally can do when she's really upset. Layla will support her if she tells Miss Balogun that she wants a better part, she knows it. And Miss Balogun is pretty kind – maybe she'll understand if Tally can find the words to tell her how she really feels.

Tally opens her mouth to speak and then a screwed-up piece of paper flies across the room and lands at her feet. Miss Balogun straightens up and glares at the rest of the class.

"Who threw this?" she demands. "You're all supposed to be writing the date in your book, not wasting my time and school resources."

"It was Luke!" calls out one of the kids from the back.

Miss Balogun looks at him enquiringly. "Well?"

"Sorry, Miss," he replies. "I just wanted to send a note to Tally saying that I think she'll be really good at the lights and stuff."

Miss Balogun's eyes soften and she smiles at him. "That's a lovely thought, if slightly poorly executed," she says. "Pick it up then, Tally. And have you come to a decision about the production?"

Tally bends down and picks up the piece of paper. Then she looks at Miss Balogun and nods.

"I'll be fantastic at the lights, and me and Miles will make a good team," she tells her, echoing the teacher's earlier words. "Yes. I'll do it."

Miss Balogun's face shines as if Tally has flicked a switch and turned on ten spotlights.

"Fantastic!" she declares. "That's all sorted then!" She spins away and heads back to the front of the room. "Now then, everybody, today's lesson is all about using descriptive language to engage the reader."

Holding her hands underneath the desk so that she can't be seen, Tally uncrumples the piece of paper and then pulls it towards her so that she can read what's on it.

It is not a note of congratulations. Not that this is a surprise to her, but even so, the hatred that springs off the page makes her blink.

Tell anyone that you saw me in the cloakroom, and I'll make your life hell, Weirdo Adams.

Tally screws it back up and shoves it to the back of her desk drawer. She could show it to Miss Balogun, but what would be the point of that? Luke seems to have convinced their teacher that he is perfect, and Tally knows that once adults make their mind up about you, it's almost impossible to tell them who you really are. It's the same with Mum and Dad. They've decided that she's a problem, and now they're going to take her to a head doctor who probably won't listen to her either. Nobody ever listens to her – so she's going to stop talking and start showing them what they want to see, starting now.

No more playing Peaches and Shadow games at lunchtime.

No more letting them see how much it hurts when they upset her.

No more giving her opinion, even when she knows that she's right and that her ideas are the best.

No giving anyone a chance to call her *weird* or *broken* or *bad*.

She has three problems, but she only needs one solution.

Tally Olivia Adams is going to be the best person that she can possibly be, and show everyone that she's a *nice, normal girl* with nothing even a little bit wrong.

She's going to give them the Tally they want to see.

And they're going to stop thinking of her as some kind of *different*.

WHO PEOPLE WANT ME TO BE
VS WHO I REALLY AM

They want me to fit into their little square box – but my personality is the wrong shape for that.

They want me to sit still to show that I'm listening – but I listen best when my body is jiggling and moving.

They expect me to cope when something unexpected happens – but I need warning if things are going to change.

They think I shouldn't mind when something goes a bit wrong – but a bit wrong to them is the end of the world to me.

They'd prefer it if I only ever said nice things – instead of what I'm actually feeling.

They want me to be like them – but I'm only like me.

CHAPTER 10

"Let's go! Ameet – you're on first, OK?" Luke's voice rings across the playground.

Layla grabs hold of Tally's hand and pulls her forward. "Just one game," she pleads with her. "One game of *Infection*, that's all. It'll be fun!"

Tally glances around. The yard is filled with kids, most of who seem to be shrieking or running or chasing after a football. It's noisy and chaotic, and the last thing she wants to do is join in.

"If we stick together, we can beat the boys," says Lucy, sprinting up to where they're standing, with Ayesha close behind her. "Ayesha and I will guard each other and you two can do the same."

Tally doesn't want to guard anyone, not even Layla. What she really wants is to find a quiet place where she can give her brain a break, just for one minute. Miss Balogun has had them doing practice test papers all morning, and there's been no time to do anything except think, think, think. Right now, she needs a moment to remember how to breathe properly.

"I think I might go—" she starts.

"—Just *play the game*, won't you?" snaps Lucy, slightly impatiently. "We're *all* playing, so why won't you? Why do you always have to be different?"

Tally swallows hard and looks down at the ground. Her school shoes are all scuffed up around the toes from where she spent yesterday break-time kneeling down to rescue the woodlice that appeared at the start of the play trail and that could have easily been trampled on by the little kids' feet. She had intended on going back there today, just to check that they were still safely in the pile of leaves where she put them.

But Lucy is right. If she wants to be like them then she has to join in.

She has to play the game.

Taking a deep breath, a bit like she does when she's about to dive into the swimming pool, Tally nods at Lucy.

"Here we go!" yells Ameet. "If I catch you then you're one of the Infected and you have to hunt the others."

"Run, Tally!" screeches Layla, letting go of her hand and dashing away.

Tally hesitates for a second and then sees Ameet heading straight towards her. She doesn't have a choice and Layla said it would be fun.

She can do this.

Layla lied.

Tally runs, but no matter where she turns, there is always someone close behind her, chasing her down. She twists around corners and ducks behind other kids, but they're relentless in their pursuit, and the longer she runs, the more of them seem to be chasing her. She can't see Layla anywhere – all she can see is the blurred shapes of people either hunting her or hindering her escape.

And the noise. The sound of people howling her name like a pack of wolves makes the hairs on the back of her neck stand on end. She wants to stop and hide, but she can't because they're snapping at her heels and she mustn't let them catch her. She can't become infected, she just can't. That isn't OK, even if it is only pretend.

And so she keeps on running.

"Tally!"

She can hear the voice over the pounding of her feet, but she keeps going.

"Tally!"

It's louder now, and a second later a hand grabs her arm and pulls her to a halt. She twists in their grip, ready to lurch away, and then sees Layla grinning at her.

"You can stop running now!" Layla tells her. "It's time to go in."

Tally blinks and looks around. The rest of the school are starting to line up, ready to go back into the building while most of year six are standing behind Layla and staring at her.

Tally braces herself for the inevitable taunts and horrid comments and jibes, but they don't appear. Instead, people are smiling and nodding, and at the back of the crowd, Lucy and Ayesha are laughing and giving each other high-fives.

"Line up please, year six!" calls Mrs Bernard, the new lunchtime supervisor.

"You're so fast," says Ameet as everyone starts to walk towards the school. "I didn't know you could run."

Tally shrugs. "I can run if I have to."

"How come you never win on sports day, then?" asks someone else.

Tally shrugs. "I guess it's different if you're being chased," she mumbles.

She doesn't know what just happened, but she does know that she wasn't running for fun – she was running to escape.

"You won the game!" says Lucy as they make their way up the stairs and into class. "That's totally going to stop Luke from saying that girls can't win *Infection*."

"Yeah, you're super fast!" adds Ayesha. "You're our secret weapon!"

Tally walks towards her desk, the smiles and praise from the rest of the class washing over her like a huge wave.

She did it.

She did what everyone else was doing and it actually *worked*.

And if the happy feeling isn't quite enough to silence the unwelcome voice in her head, the one that is whispering that they only like her because she did what they wanted her to do, then she's just going to have to do her best to ignore it.

Even when it repeats Ayesha's words in a hissing, sneaky kind of way.

You're our secret weapon.

She isn't a weapon and she isn't a secret. She's just her – the same her that she's always been. Although it's definitely true that everyone prefers her when she's being a slightly different version of *her*.

A better version of *her*.

"Let's play again tomorrow," calls Ameet as Miss Balogun walks into the classroom. "You have to play too, Tally!"

Tally nods and pulls out her newest pencil case, smiling to herself. What's happened in the past doesn't matter. It's the present that counts, and right now she's part of something good.

She can be *this* Tally.

This Tally does what everyone else does, because if she's learnt one thing since she started in year six, it's that nobody likes it when you're different. Different people don't get the main part in the production and they don't get lots of friends.

Being different never brings anything but trouble and bad luck.

It's time to fit in and show everyone just how much like them she can be.

CHAPTER 11

Tally listens to the laughter coming from the other side of the door. It's quiet and she has to strain to hear it, but she knows they're all in there, having fun without her. She counts to five and then turns the handle, pushing the door open to reveal Mum, Dad and Auntie Tish all staring back at her.

"Oh, Tally," sighs Mum. "What is it this time? You've already had a glass of water and I've been up three times. You need to go to bed."

Tally frowns. "I can't sleep," she says accusingly. "You're all being too loud."

Dad opens his mouth to speak but Mum beats him to it.

"Then we'll be a bit quieter," she says. "Now up you go. It's late."

"Goodnight, Tally." Auntie Tish raises an eyebrow. "*Again*."

Dad pushes back his chair and gets up. "I'll tuck you in," he says, putting his hand gently on Tally's back and guiding her out of the room. "There'll be plenty of time to see Auntie Tish tomorrow. She's staying the whole weekend."

Tally knows this. She also knows that Mum and Dad spent last night arguing about the fact that Auntie Tish announced yesterday afternoon that her weekend plans had fallen through and so she'd be visiting with them. Mum said that it would have been nice to have been asked rather than told, which Tally thought was a bit ironic.

Anyway, she's not that bothered about seeing Auntie Tish and it's certainly not the reason that she keeps getting out of bed. There's just something not right about having to go to sleep when everyone else is awake and having a good time. It makes Tally feel panicky inside as if life is whizzing past and she's just wasting it in bed. Then again, the last thing she wants is to be the only person awake in the house. That's a terrifying thought and it's the reason she usually asks Mum or Dad to stay in her room until she's fallen asleep. Tally thinks that being the only person awake at night is a bit like being the only person in the world – it's lonely and empty and frightening.

"Will you stay here with me?" she asks Dad as he pulls the duvet over her and picks Billy up off the floor. "Just for a bit?"

Dad shakes his head. "I can't leave your mother alone with Auntie Tish," he tells her. "Who knows what she'll end up saying? She'll probably ask her when she's going to get a proper grown-up name or something else equally offensive."

"Please." Tally's voice is quiet and Dad groans before perching on the end of her bed.

"Fine. But just for a few minutes and you need to promise to go to sleep, OK?"

Tally snuggles down and for a few moments, the room is silent. Then Tally has a thought.

"What do you mean about Auntie Tish's name? What's wrong with it?"

Dad chuckles quietly. "Well, Tish is my big sister and it's what I called her when I was little. Her real name is Patricia, but I couldn't say that so I called her Tish and then it just stuck. Your mother says it sounds like a sneeze, not a name."

Tally thinks about it.

Mum kind of has a point.

★

"Rise and shine, sleepyhead!"

Tally opens her eyes to see Mum throwing back the curtains. She instantly closes her eyes again and pulls the duvet up over her head.

"I'm tired," she groans. "I need to sleep."

"You should have gone to bed earlier, then," says Mum. "We're going for a walk in the country park with Auntie Tish and you need to get up."

"No." Tally burrows deeper down. "I need to learn my Little Red lines for the school production."

"Yes." Mum flings back the covers. "Come on. Nell is already up and dressed. And the production isn't for a month or so – you've got plenty of time to work on your star performance!"

Tally opens one eye and looks at Mum's face. She knows that it's pointless trying to argue with her when she's in this kind of a mood. She also knows that Mum wants her to be less like her and more like her sister.

Mum probably wishes that she'd had two of Nell and none of Tally.

"Fine." Tally swings her legs out of bed and sits up. "I'll get up. Just like Nell."

Mum looks confused for a moment and then she gives

Tally a big smile. "Wonderful! I'll see you downstairs for some breakfast in a few minutes."

She sweeps out of the room and Tally flops back on to the mattress. She wants to please Mum, but she really *is* tired and going for a walk in the country park is definitely not what she wants to do today. And maybe she wasn't entirely telling the truth when she told her family that she got the main part in the production, but she wasn't lying when she said that she wanted to work on her lines. She needs to be ready to leap into the role of Little Red when Miss Balogun finally sees that Tally is the right choice and will do a far better job than Carrie ever could.

If she's going to make everything right, though, then she has to do what they all want. If she's going to show them that there's nothing wrong with her, then she has to be "normal", which apparently is being just like her sister.

And how hard can that be? Nell isn't that special.

In the kitchen, Auntie Tish is sitting at the table clasping a large mug of coffee.

"Sit by me," she says, patting the chair next to her. Tally hates the smell of coffee so even though she's working hard to be like Nell, she pretends not to notice and instead slides into a seat on the opposite side of the table.

"Here's your toast," says Mum, putting a plate down in front of her.

Tally stares at the toast and then up at Mum.

"But it's Saturday," she says. "I always have a croissant on Saturday."

Mum shakes her head. "Not today, I'm afraid. I didn't get a chance to go to the bakery yesterday, so it'll have to be toast this morning."

Tally's shoulders slump. She knows why Mum couldn't go to the bakery because she heard her moaning at Dad and telling him that she'd spent the entire day cleaning the house so that it would meet his sister's high standards.

"I only got up because I thought it was a croissant," she says quietly. "I've been looking forward to it all week."

"Ooh, who's a little princess?" croons Auntie Tish, in a singsong kind of voice. "Only getting out of bed for a croissant, hey? Your mum and dad will have to pay you to get up before too long!"

Tally frowns. She would never ask her parents to give her money just for getting out of bed. And she didn't ask for the croissant, actually. Mum started it as a Saturday tradition for them all. It's not like Tally goes around demanding stuff all the time.

"We'll have croissants next week," says Mum, ignoring

Auntie Tish's comment. "Would you like peanut butter or strawberry jam on your toast?"

"Marmalade," answers Tally.

Marmalade is what Nell always chooses.

Auntie Tish makes a huffing sound and the rest of breakfast takes place in silence.

Things don't improve once the breakfast things are all put away. Dad strides into the room with Nell just behind him and claps his hands.

"Is everyone ready to go? Because we need to hurry up if we're going to get in a walk before lunch. I've booked us a table at the restaurant for one o'clock."

"Give me five minutes," says Auntie Tish. "I've just got to get my boots from my car."

"Good idea," says Dad. "Girls – you need to put on your wellies. It's probably going to be pretty muddy."

Tally stays where she is.

Nell takes her wellington boots from by the back door and grabs her old coat.

Tally doesn't move.

Mum finds her wallet and phone and then the three of them head out into the hallway.

Tally remains very, very still.

"Everyone ready?" calls Dad.

Three voices confirm that they are.

One voice is silent.

"Tally?" Mum walks back into the kitchen. "Come on! Dad's got your boots ready on the front porch."

"I'm not wearing wellies," Tally tells her. "They feel wrong on my feet."

Mum laughs but it isn't a real laugh. It sounds brittle, like something is about to snap.

"Don't be silly," she says. "You don't want to get your trainers muddy, do you? It'll make a complete mess of them."

"No," agrees Tally. "But I won't, because I'm not going in any mud. And I'm not silly."

"What's going on?" asks Dad, marching into the room. "We're going to be late."

"Tally doesn't want to wear her wellies," Mum informs him. "Apparently they feel wrong."

"It's the first I've heard of it," says Dad, frowning. "You wore them a few weeks ago when we went down to the beach."

"That was on sand," Tally explains. "They feel OK on sand."

"That really isn't a logical argument to make," Dad tells her.

Tally shrugs. She doesn't know what else to say. She just knows that she can't wear the boots and she can't walk in mud – not unless she wants to feel absolutely horrible for the rest of the day, and that is not an option because she's trying to show them that she can be normal and good and she can't possibly do that if she's feeling awful inside.

"Just wear your trainers, then," sighs Mum, glancing at the clock. "We'll deal with the mess later."

"No!" Tally stands up and faces them. "And stop saying that word!"

Mum and Dad look at each other like they haven't got a clue what she's talking about, like the word *mess* doesn't make them feel gross and squirmy and itchy inside.

"What's the problem?" Auntie Tish is standing in the doorway. "Are we going or not?"

"We'll be with you in a minute," says Mum. "Just give us a second."

Auntie Tish doesn't move.

"Are you letting this one rule the roost again?" she asks, her voice as slippery as an eel. "I'd have thought you'd have put your foot down by now, Kevin."

"Just leave it, Tish," says Dad, turning to face her. "You're not helping."

Auntie Tish makes a noise in the back of her throat. "It's the two of *you* who aren't helping yourselves," she says. "Honestly, I just think you need to lay down the law with this girl."

Mum's face flushes a deep red colour. "You don't understand," she murmurs, almost as if she's talking to herself.

Auntie Tish sighs. "I'm just concerned that this is all getting out of hand," she says, her voice all sweetness now. It reminds Tally of the time she ate too many sherbet Dib-Dabs and made herself feel sick. "This friction can't be healthy for any of you. If you don't stop letting her get away with this behaviour then you're going to have a real problem on your hands. She's turning into a nightmare."

Tally grips the edge of the table as hard as she can.

She has nightmares all the time and they're terrifying, dark, unsettling things. How can Auntie Tish say that about her?

"She's our daughter," says Mum and when Tally looks at her, Mum's eyes are as steely as her voice. "And I don't appreciate your comments."

"And your name sounds like a sneeze," murmurs Tally, backing her mother up. "Mum thinks so too."

"It just makes me so worried for you all." Auntie

Tish shakes her head sadly. "You love those children too much, Kevin."

"Hey!" Dad frowns at Auntie Tish. "Don't bring Nell into this. She's done nothing wrong."

Tally isn't sure what to think about this comment, but the conversation is moving too quickly for her to give it much thought.

"Of course not." Auntie Tish gives him a wary smile. "But just imagine what their grandparents would think if they could see them now. They'd be horrified at the way you let the children make the rules."

"Because they clearly did such a good parenting job with you?" snarls Mum. "And don't you *dare* tell us that we love our children *too much*."

Dad steps in between them.

"OK, let's all calm down," he says, holding his hands in the air like he's stopping traffic.

"I'm completely calm." Auntie Tish shrugs her shoulders. "I'm just saying that if Tally spent two days in *my* house living under *my* rules, then she wouldn't behave like this."

The rushing noise is so loud in Tally's ears that for a second she thinks that there must be a storm brewing. Then she blinks and realizes that there *is* a storm on the way but it's not outside. It's inside her head and it's trying to escape.

"You have no right to say something like that." Mum steps forward and pulls Tally close to her. "You have no idea what the situation is like here – you've been in this house for less than twenty-four hours and suddenly you're an expert on my child? You don't understand what we're going through here."

The wind picks up and the thunder-clouds gather. Anyone with any sense would run for cover.

Auntie Tish sniffs loudly. "I didn't say that I was an expert, but the situation is quite obvious. Tally clearly has no barriers and you both give in to her every demand."

Lightning flashes like a warning signal. Tally plants her feet on the ground and tries to remember how to breathe. She just has to ignore the words and remember her plan.

Be good. Be good. Be good.

"I'm merely trying to help," explains Auntie Tish. "This overparenting is creating a monster."

The sky rips itself in two and there is nothing that Tally can do about it except let the storm break.

I am not a nightmare.

Chairs fly through the air.

I am not a monster.

Plates crash to the ground.

Nell appears in the doorway and clings on to the doorframe while the hurricane hurls itself around the kitchen.

I am me I am me I am me I am me.

Tally doesn't see when Auntie Tish leaves the room and she doesn't hear the sound of the front door slamming as she stomps off to her car, her hastily packed bag held in one hand. She doesn't notice Nell righting the chairs or Dad picking up the pieces of broken crockery and putting them in the bin.

She only knows that Mum is holding her tightly, both of them sitting on the kitchen floor with Mum's arms wrapped around her, waiting for the storm to blow itself out.

"I tried really hard to do what you wanted," she whispers eventually, once the shaking has stopped. "Did you see me trying?"

Mum squeezes her a bit tighter. "I did," she tells her.

"It's just really hard," Tally murmurs. "And when Auntie Tish said those things, it made me forget that I was supposed to be like Nell today."

Mum shifts a little so that she can look at Tally's face. "I don't want you to be like Nell," she says. "I want you to be *you*."

Tally closes her eyes as a wave of exhaustion washes over her. She wants to believe Mum, she really does. But if it was OK to be *her* then they wouldn't be trying so hard to fix her, would they? If it was OK to be her, everyone wouldn't keep getting so mad at her all the time.

I am not a nightmare.

I am not a monster.

But I don't know who I'm supposed to be.

Trouble – Dad says it's my middle name.

Always messing stuff up even though I don't mean to.

Labelled naughty, difficult, challenging, oversensitive.

Like they've opened up a dictionary and chosen all the bad words.

Yet inside, I'm just Tally.

CHAPTER 12

"Can we *please* dim the lights?" Miss Balogun's voice floats across the hall.

Tally blinks and looks up.

"Tally!" Miles reaches across and pulls down the switch on the light board. "Miss Balogun has called you three times! You have to focus on the script or I'm not going to let you do any of the cool stuff."

"I *am* focusing on the script," Tally retorts. "Look!" She brandishes the tattered booklet in the air, some of the pages curling at the corners. "I've read it all the way through about five hundred times."

"Why would you do that?" Miles looks down at the switchboard, his face screwed up in confusion. "Five hundred is a *lot*. Like, it could be a new world record for the number of times a person has read the script of *Little*

Red – The Untold Tale."

Tally shakes her head. She is not in the mood for yet another conversation about ridiculous world records, not today.

"And – action!" calls Miss Balogun and the hall descends into silence. The curtains swish open and Carrie tentatively makes her way on to the stage.

"Tally – the spotlight!" hisses Miles.

Tally frowns and hesitates, wondering what would happen if she didn't push the switch. It's actually quite nice sitting here with Miles when it's quiet and dark. Maybe school would be a little more bearable if they could sit like this for a little while every day. Invisible and unwatched and unjudged, just for a few moments.

And then Miles presses the button that starts the music and Carrie's nervous voice stutters in the darkness, and Tally knows that she doesn't have a choice. She leans forward and moves the switch up, up, up until Carrie is bathed in light, her voice growing and swelling in volume and confidence as Tally increases the intensity of the spotlight.

The song ends and the room erupts in applause.

"Carrie!" exclaims Miss Balogun, walking forward. "Where on earth did that performance come from? I knew that you could sing, but we haven't heard anything like that from you before."

It's true. They've been rehearsing for a few weeks, and while Carrie knows all her lines, she's been quiet and unsure.

Carrie smiles, her cheeks flushed.

"I think it must be my lucky charm."

"What lucky charm?" asks Lucy.

Carrie's face lights up. "My aunt came to visit at the weekend," she tells them. "She's really lovely! And I told her about how I'd got the main part in the production but that I kept feeling really nervous. She told me that the same thing used to happen to her when she had to do any speaking in front of people."

Tally scowls. Of course Carrie's *lovely* aunt came to stay this weekend. And of course there's no way that she'd have a relative as mean as Auntie Tish. It took two whole days for Tally to feel a bit calmer about the things that were said about her, and while Mum and Dad were nice and let her watch her programmes for most of the weekend, she knows that they've been talking about what happened. And that appointment with the head doctor is getting closer.

Carrie carried on. "But when she was younger, my

mum gave her a lucky charm. And now my aunt's given it to me, and it totally works! Look!"

She reaches into her pocket and pulls out a delicate silver chain, and the whole class, including Tally, leans forward to take a closer look.

"Why have you got a necklace with a bug on it?" asks Ameet.

"It's a ladybird," says Carrie. "They're supposed to bring good luck, and if I keep this on me at all times then my aunt says that I'll be a star!"

"Did you know that the largest collection of ladybird items in the world is owned by a woman in Ukraine?" whispers Miles. "She's got five thousand, five hundred and fifty-five ladybird related things, including a mobile phone in the shape of a ladybird *and* a vacuum cleaner."

"How on earth would I know that?" hisses Tally back to him. "And stop saying the word *ladybird*. They're actually beetles."

Miss Balogun smiles at Carrie. "Well, I'm not sure if it was the lucky necklace or the fact that this is our first performance using the lights on the stage, but whatever the reason, you were very good!"

"We aren't allowed jewellery in class." Tally raises her voice so that they can all hear her. "It's a school rule."

A groan echoes around the hall and a few people shoot Tally a dark look.

"Why do you always have to spoil everything?" mutters one of Carrie's friends and the others murmur in agreement.

Miss Balogun clears her throat. "Tally is right. But while we do have a ban on jewellery in school, I think in this case we can make an exception as long as it stays in Carrie's desk tray when we're not rehearsing."

Tally sinks back into her chair. It's so unfair. A girl like Carrie doesn't need a lucky charm. She's already got quite enough luck. And what's the point in having rules if they can just be broken whenever people feel like it? Why does she try so hard to keep them if nobody even cares about them in the first place?

"Are we going to do my dance number now?" asks Lucy. "I've been working really hard on it."

Miss Balogun nods. "In a moment, Lucy. I just want Carrie to know how very impressive she's just been." She turns towards the side of the hall where Tally and Miles are huddled on chairs behind the light and sound boards. "Can we have the full lights back on please?" Then she turns back to Carrie and continues to tell her how her singing is going to blow the audience away.

Tally leans back in her chair and folds her arms.

"What about telling us how impressive we've been?" she mutters. "If it wasn't for the brilliant lights, then Carrie couldn't have performed like that – Miss Balogun literally just said that it was because of the lights but there's no praise for us, is there?"

Miles turns on the main lights and starts making notes on his already detailed lighting plan. "Why does it matter to you so much? Who cares?"

Tally's head snaps round so fast that it hurts her neck. "*I* care! And so should you. How can you think it's OK for us to be stuck here getting no attention or thanks while everyone else gets to be in the spotlight?" She exhales loudly. "The spotlight that I'm over here making, by the way."

Miles shrugs. "I like being over here," he tells her. "It's quite nice staying out of the drama."

"But don't you just want to be like everyone else?" Tally asks. "Aren't you sick of being different and alone all the time?"

Miles stares at the space to the side of Tally's head, his face screwed up as he contemplates her words.

"I like being on my own," he says eventually. "And I don't think I'm any more *different* than everybody else is.

We're all different, aren't we? It's not a thing."

Tally doesn't know what to say to him. Because yes, of course it's a *thing*. Being different is definitely a *thing*, and she doesn't know how Miles can be so casual about it.

Or not know just how different he is to the rest of them.

"And how can I be like everybody else, when nobody is the same?" he continues. "I'm just me. That's the only person I know how to be."

Tally picks up her script and opens it again to Little Red's big speech. She's almost got the whole thing completely memorized, but there's just one part that she's struggling to get right. It comes just after the wolf has told Little Red that it's hard when everyone thinks you're a fierce, bad monster, but really you just feel scared and lonely. When Luke reads the lines it takes every bit of control that Tally possesses not to snort – as if a boy like *him* would ever know how it feels to be scared and alone.

"Let's work on the dance scene now!" calls Miss Balogun. "Lucy – we'll have you at the back of the stage to begin with and then you can dance forwards to join the others. Tech crew – let's go!"

Miles starts the music and the hall is filled with the sound of several pairs of year six feet stomping about on the wooden floor.

"You can just be *you*, you know?" Miles's voice is quiet, but Tally can still hear him. "It's OK. You don't have to be like anyone else."

She looks up from the script, the stamping feet and the loud music making it feel like they're in their own little bubble where nobody can hear them. And maybe it's this that makes her mouth open and words that she's only ever thought about come trickling out.

"I don't know if I want to be me," she tells him. "Not when nothing ever works out for me and I never get any good luck. I think it might all be a bit easier if I *wasn't* me."

And then she returns to the script, already regretting telling him anything. He can't possibly understand what it feels like to be her – constantly working to figure out how she's supposed to be behaving and what she's supposed to be saying. If he knew, then there's no way he'd ever say something as stupid as it's OK to be her.

Or that it's OK to be different.

CHAPTER 13

"So if you're all ready, I want you to get into your science groups and begin the experiment." Miss Balogun claps her hands and gives the class a nod. "Let's try to keep the noise to a minimum, yes?"

Layla stands up and starts walking towards the back of the room. Tally waits a moment, reluctant to follow. Miss Balogun has swapped the science groups around, and now she and Layla have to work with Luke and Ameet. Things have been a bit better at school since Tally started playing *Infection* every break and lunchtime but she doesn't trust Luke and sometimes she sees him glaring at her, even though she hasn't done anything wrong.

"Come on, Tally!" calls Layla. "We've got to decide what shape to make the plasticine."

Tally swallows a sigh and plasters a smile on to her

face. She can do this. She's good at science, and maybe if she shows Luke how much she knows then he'll stop being so unfriendly.

"Hey, Ameet – catch!"

As Tally approaches the table, she sees Luke throw their ball of plasticine across the table towards his friend. Ameet laughs as the sticky lump flies through the air, and when he picks it up, Tally can see that it's covered in fluff and dirt from the classroom floor.

"Stop messing about," says Layla. "We're supposed to be investigating what shape has the most water resistance."

The boys ignore her.

"Look what I've made!" crows Ameet, brandishing the plasticine in front of them. "It's a chicken!"

"That's not a chicken," scoffs Luke, grabbing it off him. "But look at what I can make."

Tally watches as he pulls and kneads and manipulates the disgusting piece of plasticine with his fingers. She makes a silent promise not to touch it. She usually likes squishy things – she's got an entire collection of squishy toys at home – but this piece of grotty plasticine is making her tummy flip over.

"Ta-dah!" Luke holds up his creation. It's got a head,

a body, two arms and two legs, but that's where any resemblance to a person ends. He's added two tiny blob eyes and pressed his fingernail deep into the face to make a slash-like smile. The whole thing looks horrific and freakish. "Guess who it is!"

Ameet starts laughing again. "The creature from the black lagoon? The stuff of my nightmares? Mate – that is so weird!"

"You're close," Luke tells him, shooting Tally a quick glance. "And it's *definitely* weird. Weirdo Adams, in fact."

He tosses the awful model to Tally, whose hands reach out to catch it before her brain can tell them not to. "There you go. A little present for you."

"Luke!" snaps Layla. "If you don't stop being so stupid then I'm telling Miss Balogun. Can we please just get on with the investigation?"

Luke shrugs. "Sure. I was only having a laugh."

Ameet steps forwards and picks up a plastic container. "I'll go and get some water," he tells them. "You guys start making the first shape, yeah? Then we can time how long it takes to sink."

"We have to write down the method first," Layla tells them. "We should do that before we get the water."

The three of them sit down and open their science

books. Tally stays where she is, staring down at the grotesque model in her hands.

"Come on, Tally," says Layla, looking up at her. "If we don't finish the task then we'll have to stay in at lunchtime."

"Yeah," agrees Ameet. "Hurry up."

Tally carefully places the plasticine doll on the table and sits next to Layla.

"It was just a daft joke," her best friend whispers, as Luke picks it up. "Just ignore him."

Tally nods as he squishes the plasticine Tally between his fingers. She keeps nodding as her body crumples and squidges and disappears, becoming a normal lump of plasticine again, just like all the others.

She hated that gross, dirty plasticine figure and she thinks she might hate Luke. So why does it make her head buzz and her tummy swirl to see him destroying it?

And why does it feel like it's her that Luke is squishing into a different shape?

"I'm so tired," moans Lucy as they walk down the stairs, the science lesson thankfully over. "My dance class went late last night, and I've got to go to another one after school."

"Maybe you shouldn't bother going," says one of the other year six girls in a sneaky voice. "You can't be very good if you have to practise so much!"

Her friends start sniggering. "Yeah – maybe you should start a new hobby. Like reading or baking or something that doesn't involve having good coordination skills!"

Ayesha grabs hold of Lucy's arm protectively.

"Don't listen to them," she says, shooting a glare at the girl who spoke first. "They're just trying to upset you."

Lucy pulls her arm away and tosses her long hair over one shoulder. "Like I'd let any of *them* bother me!" she snorts. "They're just jealous that I get to have a dance solo in the production and they're stuck in the chorus."

Tally watches as the girls wrinkle up their noses and stalk ahead, muttering furiously to each other. Lucy has never been afraid to say what she thinks, but nobody ever tells her that she shouldn't say what's on her mind.

Lucy makes being in year six look easy.

"Are you playing *Infection* today?" asks Ayesha as they all head outside. The weather is warmer now, and even though it's only the start of May, there's a hint of summer in the air.

Tally nods. She seems to be doing quite a lot of nodding these days, but it's an easy way to make people pleased with her, and she's started to realize that a lot of the time they don't actually want to hear what she has to say. They just want to know that she agrees with what they're saying.

"Are you all right?" asks Layla, as Lucy and Ayesha run off to the far side of the playground. "I know Luke upset you with that stupid plasticine doll, but he was just being silly. Don't let it get to you."

Tally gives a little laugh. "I'm not bothered," she tells Layla. "As if I'd let someone like *him* upset me! He's just jealous of me."

Layla gives Tally a confused look, but before she can speak, Lucy is racing back towards them. "Ayesha is *Infected!*" she screams. "Run!"

The girls scatter across the playground. Tally starts to run but then she remembers the look on Luke's face when he squished up the fake Tally model and her legs stop working. She can't just stand still and wait to be infected, though. She needs to find somewhere safe to go, but that's the problem with school.

Nowhere is safe for a girl like her.

"Are you doing OK there?" asks a voice, and when Tally looks up she sees Mrs Bernard, one of the lunchtime supervisors, standing next to her. "You look like you could do with a bit of peace and quiet."

Tally stares at her. Some peace and quiet would be great, and she knows that Mrs Bernard is quite new and everything but it's hard to see how she hasn't noticed the extreme lack of both those things in the school playground.

"Your name is Tally, isn't it?" asks Mrs Bernard. "I've seen you racing around the playground with all your friends. You're a very fast runner."

Tally shrugs. They aren't all her friends and she's only fast because she has to be, but she can't say either of those things to this lady. She'd never get it.

"I was wondering if you might like to join Koala Club?" Mrs Bernard smiles at Tally. "I've been given the job of running the school library, but it's too much for just one person. I've already got a couple of kids helping me out and I thought you might be interested."

"What's Koala Club?" Tally moves closer to the wall as Ameet screeches past with Ayesha chasing right behind him. Mrs Bernard steps to the side, keeping her distance from Tally but blocking her from Ayesha's view.

"It's a club for anyone who needs a little alone time," she explains. "Just like koalas. They would rather hug a tree than hug another person, which I think is a bit like hugging a book."

Tally frowns. Mrs Bernard seems like she's a nice person, but everything she's saying is confusing.

"What I mean is that, sometimes, people need a bit of time-out," says the lunchtime supervisor, seeing the look on Tally's face. "And a library full of books is the perfect place to escape to. You can either help out by putting the returned books back on to the shelves or just curl up in the armchair and lose yourself in a story. Miles is in there today, but I'm sure he'd be happy to share the space with you, especially if you're both being quiet."

Tally shakes her head. Mrs Bernard has made Koala Club sound quite wonderful, but she can't join. Not if it's for kids like no-friends loner Miles. It's all right for him – he doesn't care what anyone thinks of him and he doesn't even want to have friends – but it's different for Tally.

She's trying to fit in, not stand out.

Which means that she can't escape to the peaceful library. She has to do her hiding in plain sight.

The First Five Words You See
Describe Who You Are!

n	o	i	s	y	g	r	o	s	s	m	z	k	l	d
s	t	r	o	n	g	z	u	a	r	t	y	m	c	p
n	k	i	n	d	s	q	o	f	a	y	u	d	h	e
q	w	n	s	p	o	r	t	y	n	z	o	y	a	x
w	e	i	r	d	z	b	o	l	d	b	f	r	t	q
a	m	a	z	i	n	g	h	y	n	o	r	u	t	p
h	k	e	g	j	l	v	e	w	x	s	e	p	y	a
e	x	c	i	t	a	b	l	e	n	s	a	r	o	h
t	p	g	f	c	m	l	p	w	j	y	k	s	h	y
c	a	r	i	n	g	w	f	y	p	k	e	f	d	z
r	v	g	n	y	s	t	u	b	b	o	r	n	q	f
u	f	b	d	u	q	r	l	s	a	n	u	j	f	p
d	l	o	i	r	t	c	o	n	f	i	d	e	n	t
e	m	n	m	u	s	i	c	a	l	h	r	y	b	m
q	w	o	r	r	i	e	d	r	t	h	s	l	o	w

I did this word search after my rubbish day at school. I guess I shouldn't be surprised that the first five words that leapt out at me were: freak, gross, stubborn, worried and weird. I also saw: kind, amazing, caring and musical but you're only allowed five so they don't count.

CHAPTER 14

It's Saturday morning, and that means one thing in the Adams household. Chores time. It's been this way as long as Tally can remember, and only a major disaster or emergency (like an unexpected visit from Auntie Tish) can change the schedule. The good news on this particular Saturday is that Auntie Tish is nowhere to be seen. The bad news is that means the chores still have to happen.

Tally eats her croissant slowly, enjoying the buttery taste and the sensation of the flaky pastry on her tongue. Her main task this morning is to tidy her room, which is a job she normally hates. Today though, she's kind of looking forward to it. School has been completely exhausting this week – she had no idea how much effort it would be, constantly trying to be good – and even though nobody has called her "weird" (except Luke, and he doesn't count as a proper person) and she's been included in everything, she still feels drained and empty. Plus the horrible year six tests are next week, and she's dreading Monday morning.

Which is why tidying her room doesn't seem so bad. She's been thinking that she should organize all of her squishies for a while and the pile of cuddly toys on her bed is a total mess. Poor Billy is somewhere at the bottom and she fell asleep last night before she could find him. Maybe if she plays some Taylor Swift and gets her room in order, her head might feel a bit less cluttered too. She can hang out in her bedroom with nobody to bother her and just enjoy making it her own, safe space.

The thought makes a warm, happy feeling spread through her body.

Standing up, she heads across the kitchen and puts her plate on the countertop next to the empty dishwasher. She *could* put it inside, but stacking the dishwasher is one of Nell's chores and Tally doesn't see why she should make it any easier for her.

"Nice croissant?" asks Mum, walking into the room with a huge pile of laundry in her arms.

Tally nods and Mum beams. "Excellent! That should give you the energy to go and tidy your room, then."

The warm, happy feeling evaporates, like a single drop of rain on a scorching pavement. Tally can feel her heart starting to race and her fingers clench tightly as she tries to stop the feeling of dread from creeping any further up her body.

She tries. She really does try. And she might have even succeeded if Mum hadn't made it even worse.

"Off you go!" she says brightly. "The sooner you get it done, the sooner you can enjoy the weekend."

Tally stares at her. She'd been starting to think that tidying her room could be relaxing and enjoyable, but Mum has just made it super-clear that it's an undesirable chore that should be done as quickly as possible.

That's not the worst part, though. The worst part is the *being told*.

"I was just about to go and do it." The words push themselves out through Tally's gritted teeth.

"Oh…" Mum pauses for a second. "Well then, that's great! Once you've finished, I thought we could bake some cupcakes together. I've found a delicious-looking recipe that we haven't tried yet."

She just doesn't get it.

"I can't do it *now*!" mutters Tally. "Not when you've ruined it."

Mum stares back at her in astonishment. "What on earth have I ruined? You said that you were going to go and tidy your room, and I said that was great and we could bake cupcakes when you were done. How does any of that *ruin* anything?"

Tally stamps her foot in frustration. "And now you're lying!" she cries. "You told me to go and tidy my room first before you even knew what I was planning to do. And I was looking forward to it and I was going to sort all my stuff out, but now you've spoilt everything and I hate you."

Mum shakes her head and takes a deep breath. "It makes me feel very sad when you say things like that to me, Tally. I'm sorry that you hate me right now, but I love you. We can talk about this later when you're not feeling so angry."

She's using the slow voice that she always uses when she's trying to do the things they told her to do on that stupid *good parenting* course and it's. Just. Too. Much.

"Just *shut up*!" screeches Tally. "You're always making it about you, but it's not. I'm allowed to hate you if I want to – you can't stop me."

She spins on her heel and storms out of the room before Mum can see the tears that are threatening to spill from her eyes.

"I hate you, I hate you, I hate you," she hisses as she pounds up the stairs. "I hate you all and I hate everything and I'm *not* angry."

Slamming her bedroom door as loudly as she can, Tally throws herself on to her bed and curls up into the tiniest shape possible. Her heart feels like it's about to thud itself out of her chest and her legs are tingling, as if she needs to run. Reaching up, she can feel beads of sweat forming on her forehead and under her arms, and inside her mouth has suddenly gone as dry as the desert.

How can Mum say that to her? How could someone who is supposed to love her make her feel this way? Doesn't she understand how terrifying it is to be told that she's made Mum feel sad; to have that much power? It's like being on a rollercoaster, only not the kind that Tally loves. This rollercoaster keeps your body still but sends your feelings on a wild and unpredictable ride. One moment Tally was feeling unhappy because Mum had upset her, and the next it was like a double switchback and suddenly it was all *her* fault and Mum was the one feeling miserable. But she's not angry – that's totally wrong.

Tally hugs her knees up to her chest. Her veins are fizzing with such intensity that she thinks she might explode. She didn't mean to upset Mum and she doesn't hate her, not at all. She *loves* her – so much so that she doesn't know how to put it into words because there aren't enough words in the universe to describe what Mum is to Tally. She's a safe place to hide when the storm is raging, and a warm, heavy blanket when everything goes wrong. She's a steaming mug of hot chocolate when the world is cold, and the safety rope that lets Tally climb higher and catches her when she falls.

And Tally has made her sad.

But Mum doesn't understand. Tally is *not* angry.

Not that it matters either way. She always seems to hurt other people without even trying. Maybe she'll be like this for ever. Maybe it would be the safest thing for everyone if she just stayed here on her bed where she can't upset anyone ever again.

She's not angry. But she doesn't really know what she is, and when she closes her eyes there is just one word flashing in the endlessness, like a faulty neon sign.

Scared.

Pulling the duvet cover up and over her head, she burrows down into the safety of darkness. When she was younger she hated the dark; she thought that there were demons lurking in the shadows, waiting to get her. Now, though, she knows better.

She's still very, very scared. But not about make-believe monsters.

No monster under her bed could be as frightening as trying to figure out why everything she does goes so badly wrong and why, no matter how hard she tries, she's starting to think that Layla was right when she said that Tally just doesn't see things the way everyone else seems to.

She's starting to think that maybe *she* is the monster.

The rest of the weekend is quiet. Mum and Dad leave Tally alone for most of the time, and she's allowed to stay in her room where she listens to Taylor Swift and cuddles Billy and snoozes because it turns out that being scared is incredibly tiring. When she does have any energy she keeps learning the lines for the part of Little Red, and by Monday morning she has memorized every single line.

"Maybe we could bake those cupcakes after school today?" suggests Mum as they reach the school playground. "Your room is looking lovely and tidy, and it'd be something nice to look forward to after today's tests."

Tally nods. "That would be good," she lies.

She doesn't really want to bake. She liked cupcakes a few months ago, but then something changed and the thought of all that sickly sweet frosting on the top makes her stomach turn over.

Mum wants to bake them, though. And baking cupcakes with her is easier than trying to find the right words, out of the one million potential words in the English language, to tell her that she loves her and she's sorry and she never wants to make her sad ever again. Tally wants Mum to be happy more than anything.

Mum smiles.

"Good luck with the tests," she tells her. "Dad and Nell said to tell you that they're sending you good luck vibes too! Oh – and Auntie Tish!" She hands Tally her lunchbox. "Have a good day, sweetheart. I love you."

Tally's head jerks around to check that nobody has heard this embarrassing declaration, but everyone else is already heading into the building. She nods at Mum and takes two steps away before quickly turning back and grabbing Mum's hand.

Four rapid squeezes, so tight that she can feel the knuckles on Mum's hand crunching together. One squeeze for each word.

I love you too.

And then she's gone, lost in the crowd of year six kids all piling into school and talking animatedly about what questions might be on the maths test and whether it matters if they can't remember the difference between the median, mode and mean averages.

"Good luck, Tally!" says Lucy as they push their way up the stairs.

"Good luck, everyone!" says Miss Balogun a few minutes later, as she gets them all to line up at the door with their pencil cases. "Just do your best and remember to stay calm."

"Good luck!" squeals Ayesha as they get ready to walk out of the classroom, heading to the big hall where the tables are set out in rows, one for each child.

Tally moves into her position behind Miles, who turns around.

"Good luck," he says in the direction of her left shoulder. "If you believe in that kind of thing. I don't, though. You don't get a Guinness world record through good luck, that's for sure."

"Good luck to you, anyway," Tally tells him. They've started talking quite a lot during rehearsals and she's been kind of surprised to find that Miles actually has quite a lot of interesting things to say. "Hey! Did you know that the most tattooed man in the world is called—"

"— Lucky Diamond Rich," finishes Miles, grinning at the floor. "I did know that. You've been reading the book I lent you, then?"

"Maybe." Tally shrugs.

"Off we go!" calls Miss Balogun.

Tally steps forward and then hesitates. "Miss! I've forgotten my ruler!"

At the front of the line, Miss Balogun waves her hand. "Go and get one from the back of the class," she instructs her. "And then join on to the back of the line. Now – if anyone needs to go to the toilet before we make a start then I strongly suggest you use the bathroom next to the hall. There will be no chance to leave the hall once we've begun."

"Good luck, Tally," says Carrie as Tally moves out of the line. "I hope it's not going to be too difficult today – I hate tests!"

"What about if there's a fire, Miss?" Lucy's voice floats back towards Tally as the class start to move out of the room.

"If the fire alarm goes off then we will obviously follow

our fire drill procedure," Miss Balogun informs her. "You don't need to worry about that."

"What about if there's an earthquake?" calls Luke. "Are we allowed to stop the test then?"

Tally doesn't hear Miss Balogun's response, and pauses for a second to contemplate whether his question needs to be given any consideration.

"Did you know that the most powerful earthquake ever recorded was in Chile in 1960?" Miles says as he steps forward. "It had a magnitude of nine point five and killed a whole lot of people. I read that in the first *Guinness Book of World Records* that my dad gave me. It's super old and it's my most precious possession."

"Go and get a ruler," Layla tells Tally, seeing her face. "And stop worrying about earthquakes. We live in the South of England and an earthquake is highly unlikely."

Tally thinks about this and then nods.

"Be quick!" says Layla, moving towards the door. "And good luck!"

And then the room is silent, the only noise the sound of many pairs of feet walking down the stairs and away. Tally races across the room and takes a ruler from the box at the back of the class before making her way towards the door, weaving in between the desks and keen to catch up with everyone else.

And then she sees it and her feet stop still.

Good luck, good luck, good luck, good luck.

Mum, Dad, Nell and Auntie Tish, all sending her positive vibes. Tally knows that she is still the least lucky person in the universe but, still, it feels nice to have people hoping that maybe today will be different. Even if one of them *is* Auntie Tish.

Good luck, good luck, good luck.

Lucy, Miss Balogun and Ayesha, sending her thoughts of good fortune.

Good luck, good luck.

Miles and Carrie, wishing her a lucky break even if Miles didn't sound like he thought being lucky was even real.

Good luck.

Layla. Her best friend. The person who is always there for her and sees her when nobody else can.

All that luck being sent in her direction.

Miles is wrong. He has to be. Because there is only one reason that the object lying at her feet could possibly be right here, right now. There's only one reason that Tally is alone in the classroom with nobody to see her; nobody to question what she already knows she's about to do.

There's only one reason that she can reach down and pick it up, cradling it in her hands like it's worth a million pounds.

It's luck. *Her* luck. She was meant to have forgotten her ruler and she was meant to be here and she was meant to find this today. Carrie said it herself when she wished her good luck, almost like she left it here deliberately for Tally to find.

It's not really stealing when it was just lying there on the floor. She trails it from one hand to the other.

It's not really breaking the rules when everyone has been hoping that she'll have good luck. She holds it up and watches the way it catches the light.

Sometimes a person has to help make their own luck, that's what Dad says when Tally moans about being so unlucky. And *that's* what she's doing. Quickly, before she can change her mind, she slips the lucky charm ladybird necklace into her pocket and starts walking.

But she isn't just walking to the big hall. Not in her head. Her feet might be taking her towards the first day of year six tests, but her mind is taking her somewhere entirely different. Inside, she's walking towards a whole new life. A better life, where she's finally going to start being the person everyone wants her to be.

Tally Olivia Adams just found her luck, and she is one hundred per cent determined to make it start working for her.

CHAPTER 15

Tally looks out of the car window and grasps her hands around the seatbelt.

"I'm *not* going in there."

Mum unfastens her own belt and swivels to face Tally in the backseat. "We've been through this, Tally. I've already spoken to Dr Zennor on the phone and she sounds really nice. You're just going to have a chat with her."

Tally glowers at her from inside her tiger mask. She knows that she'd feel so much better if she could wear it for the appointment with the doctor, but she also knows that there's no way the doctor would understand and it'd just make her agree with Mum and Dad that there's something wrong with Tally.

"I don't care how nice she sounds. I'm not sick."

Mum frowns. "Of course you're not."

"So why are you trying to make me go in there, then?" She flings her hand out and points in the direction of the large building ahead of them, its gloomy greyness a stark contrast to the bright sunshine of the day.

Mum's face softens and she releases a long breath. "People come to hospital for lots of different reasons," she tells Tally. "Sometimes they're unwell and need help to get better, and other times they come looking for answers. And that's why we're here. To try and find out—"

"—What's wrong with me," interrupts Tally before Mum can finish her sentence. "You think there's something the matter with me and it needs to be fixed."

Mum twists away from Tally and opens the car door, stepping outside into the bright sunshine. Tally feels her stomach twist with worry, but before she can figure out what Mum is going to do next, the back door of the car opens and Mum slides on to the backseat next to her.

"Tally." Mum's hand reaches across and rests on her knee. "We don't think that there is anything wrong with you."

Tally scowls. "But you want to change me, don't you? That's why we're here. So that you can figure out what to do to make me a better person."

Mum's hand tightens on her leg. "Absolutely not! You are perfect exactly as you are and there is nothing about you that Dad and I would ever want to change, not in one million years!"

Tally turns and fixes Mum with an earnest look. "So let's just go home, then," she pleads. "I promise that I'll be good – I really do."

Mum scoots closer and slips her arm around Tally's shoulders. "It's not about you being *good*," she says quietly. "When I say that Dad and I don't want to change anything, I guess that's not entirely the truth."

Tally holds her breath. Here it comes. The moment she's been waiting for. The moment when Mum finally tells her that she's not the girl they wanted.

"We do want to change a few things – and one of those things is the way that we support you," Mum says quietly, her mouth close to the tiger mask. "We see how tricky life can sometimes be for you, and we just want to do whatever we can to help you figure yourself out. And right now we need a little bit of help with that, which is where Dr Zennor comes in."

"What if she says I'm autistic?" whispers Tally. "What will happen to me then?" Mum and Dad had sat her down last night and done an awful lot of talking about today's appointment, most of which Tally blocked out. She remembers the bit about autism though – the same word that Mum had said to Miss Balogun at parents' evening all those months ago. The same word that people say about Miles. She lay in bed afterwards, rolling the word around her tongue before deciding that it didn't sound like her at all.

"Nothing will happen to you," Mum assures her. "It's what we said last night – if Dr Zennor thinks that you might be autistic, then she'll write a report and send it to another doctor, and then that doctor will look at the report that we sent in and the ones from school and decide whether or not to make a diagnosis."

She pauses for a second. "And then we'll know. And we can make sure that you get the help you need with some things."

"I don't think I am autistic, though." Tally pulls away from Mum's arm and looks up at her. "I've been thinking about it and I think I'm just me. So this is probably all a waste of time."

Mum gives her a smile. "You are absolutely *you*. Nothing that the doctor says is going to change that. Let's go and have a chat with her and take it from there, yes?"

Tally closes her eyes. It's clear that Mum really wants her to go inside the hospital. And Tally is still feeling pretty bad about how she screamed at Mum this morning when she couldn't find her favourite purple T-shirt. It wasn't Mum's fault that it had somehow ended up underneath Tally's bed, she can see that now – even if at the time, all she could think about was that Mum was trying to get her to wear the yellow T-shirt and that was all wrong. Sometimes she feels really sorry for Mum, having to deal with a child like her – although feeling sorry usually just ends up making her even more scared and upset and shouty.

She opens her eyes and slowly pulls the mask off her head before reaching her hands down to unclick her seatbelt. Mum's face sags with relief as Tally opens the door and swings her legs out to step on to the hot tarmac of the car park. The doctor is going to look inside her head and write a report about her, but the doctor doesn't know everything. She can't possibly know that right now, Tally has the ladybird necklace tucked inside the pocket of her jeans. Her lucky charm that's going to make sure everything turns out fine. Her lucky charm that's going to help her show the doctor just how *nice* and *good* and *normal* she can be.

★

It seems to Tally that she has been sitting in the doctor's waiting room for an eternity. Mum perches next to her on the seat, flicking through the pages of a magazine that Tally knows she can't possibly be reading. She's already tried to engage Tally in a conversation about the summer production, but Tally would rather not pursue this line of conversation. She keeps intending to tell Mum and Dad that she's actually helping Miles with the sound and lights and wasn't given the part of Little Red, but every time she opens her mouth to tell the truth, she thinks about how proud of her they are and how they keep telling people about how well she's done to be given the lead role and her mouth snaps shut.

She doesn't want to take it away from them.

Or away from her.

"What's the doctor going to ask us?" Tally keeps her voice quiet so that nobody else can hear. There are only two other people here and they're sitting on the far side of the room. Well, the woman is sitting. The little boy with her is crawling under the chairs and making a noise that sounds distinctly like a train. Tally watches, envious of the way he doesn't seem to be aware that anyone else is there. She imagines it must be quite nice not having to *notice* all the time.

Mum turns another page. "She's probably going to ask about how things are at home," she says. "She just wants to get to know us a little bit."

Tally jerks her head to face Mum.

"You're not going to tell her about what I'm like, are you?" Her words come out in a rush. "You're not going to tell her about what happened when Auntie Tish was staying with us? Or about what happened when we were playing that game?"

It still hurts Tally to think about the Monopoly incident, even though it was ages ago. She likes playing family games, she really does. It's the losing that she hates. She tries, though; she tries very hard to remind herself of all the things that Mum and Dad are constantly saying when they play together.

It doesn't matter if you lose.

It's not the winning that counts – it's the taking part.

The thing is – those things just aren't true. It *does* matter if she loses, because when Tally loses a game it makes her feel like the biggest failure on the planet, and who would want to feel like that? Mum can tell her over and over again that it's only a game, but it doesn't feel that way to her. When she lost at Monopoly it made her whole body feel heavy and dull. It made her feel like she must be useless at everything. And that's why the curtains got ripped down from the wall and it's why Nell burst into tears and said that she was never playing a family game ever again – which Tally thought was even more unfair because it wasn't actually about Nell.

Nell was the winner.

"You can't tell the doctor about the things I do at home," she says urgently to Mum, gripping her arm. "That stuff is none of her business"

Mum pauses for a second and then nods. "I won't tell her," she says. "You don't need to worry – it's just going to be a nice, calm chat."

A door on the opposite wall opens and the doctor steps into the waiting room.

"Tally Adams?" she says, giving them a smile. "Sorry for the slight delay. Please come in."

She waves them forward and steps aside so that they can enter the room. Tally presses herself tightly against Mum and reminds herself not to do anything even a little bit unusual.

This is it. This is when the test is *really* going to start. This is when the *doctor* is going to decide if she's good enough.

Or if she needs fixing.

★

It is a very tired Tally who leaves the room, more than an hour later. The last ninety minutes have taken all of her energy and she isn't sure that she even has the strength to walk to the car.

"That was all right, wasn't it?" asks Mum as they head out into the sunshine. "You did really well."

Tally clamps her lips together. "Uh-hmm."

This isn't a safe place to show how she's really feeling.

"I thought Dr Zennor was lovely," continues Mum, pulling her car keys out of her bag. Tally glances at them, remembering how good it felt to scrape them down the side of the car. She can't do that now, though – for all she knows, the doctor is spying on her from one of the many hospital windows, waiting for her to mess up.

"That activity with the foam shapes looked fun!" Mum's voice is breezy as she clicks the car doors open, and Tally slides on to the back seat, yanking her tiger mask over her head. "I was tempted to come and have a go with you!"

Tally closes her eyes and tries to count to ten, just like Dad tells her to do when she can feel the volcano building up inside her body.

One, two. The foam shapes *were* quite fun. They were squidgy, just like some of her squishy toys at home, and she enjoyed the sensation of them in between her fingers.

Three, four. They smelt wrong though. Nobody else ever seems to notice, but what makes the perfect squishy is the exact right amount of squish and the right smell. Not too rubbery or plastic but definitely not scented, like those awful ones with fake strawberry or banana smell.

Five, six. The doctor had an aquarium in her room, and when she saw Tally looking, she gave her a piece of paper and a tub of colouring pencils and asked her to draw a picture of a rainbow fish, which sounded like an easy thing to do but Tally knew was actually a trick because there are loads of different species of rainbow fish and they all look different, so if Dr Zennor had really wanted her to draw one then she'd have been a little more specific. And secondly, if she were going to draw it properly then she'd need to know how the fish was feeling, because the colours on a rainbow fish change depending on their stress levels. The more stressed out they are, the brighter they think they have to shine.

Tally knows exactly how that feels.

Seven, eight. When she refused to draw a picture, the doctor showed her a picture instead. It had lots of funny-looking blob creatures, all doing different things, and the doctor asked Tally which one she thought was most like her. Tally wanted to answer correctly, she really did, but she didn't like looking at the blobs and none of them was anything like her. She pointed at one randomly though, just to keep the doctor happy and to show that she could do the right thing. The doctor seemed pleased and let Tally take a proper look at the fish while she talked to Mum.

Nine, Ten. And that's when it all went wrong.

Inside the mask, Tally's eyes flash open.

"What shall we have for tea tonight?" asks Mum as they pull out of the parking space. "You can choose."

"What's the point?" Tally jiggles her foot up and down, feeling the tiger start to stir. "You won't listen to me anyway."

Mum flicks on the indicator and turns on to the main road.

"What do you mean? Of course I'll listen to you."

The tiger stretches out first one paw and then the other, flexing its limbs ready to strike.

"Liar."

"Tally?" Mum glances at her daughter in the rear-view mirror. "Is something the matter?"

The tiger takes a deep breath and then it pounces.

"Yes, there's something the matter! You told the doctor everything, even though you promised me that you wouldn't! You're a liar and you've betrayed me and I'll never forgive you for as long as I live."

"Tally," starts Mum. "I don't—"

"Shut *up*, you stupid woman!" The scream tears itself from Tally's mouth, bounces around the car and hurtles back into her ears. "I *specifically* asked you *not* to tell her about what I'm like at home, but you did it anyway. I *heard* you! You told her about the ripped-down curtains and the broken plates and the thrown chairs and the hurting Nell and now she thinks I'm horrible and it's ALL YOUR FAULT!"

"Nobody thinks you're horrible," says Mum, manoeuvring the car safely on to the side of the road and coming to a halt. She turns off the engine and twists in her seat so that she can see Tally. "And I'm sorry that you think I betrayed you. It was important that the doctor got the whole story, though. I needed to tell her everything."

The tiger bares its teeth.

"I am not a story," it hisses. "I am just me – and

153

you lied."

Mum shakes her head and restarts the car. "Let's get home and we can talk about all of this properly."

The tiger slumps back in the seat and stares out of the window at the world outside. It wonders why everything has always got to be so very hard and filled with so much hurting.

CHAPTER 16

"That was SO hard," sighs Layla as they walk out of the hall on the fourth day of the tests. "I only managed to answer half the questions, and I think I probably got most of them wrong."

"I bet you didn't," Tally tells her loyally. "Everyone always thinks that they've done worse than they really did."

"That was a nightmare!" says Lucy, catching up with them. "I didn't even know what the first question was going on about."

"Me neither," moans Ayesha. "I just added up all the numbers and hoped for the best. How about you, Tally?"

The three girls turn to look at her enquiringly. Tally quickly runs through the list of possible responses in her head. Should she tell them that she doesn't care about the stupid tests? Or that she found the test quite easy so that they think she's clever? That's what she'd usually do, but the way they're staring at her makes her think again.

"Oh, yeah – total nightmare," she groans. "I barely answered any of the questions and I definitely got most of them wrong."

The girls nod in agreement and Tally relaxes her shoulder. It was the correct thing to say, which at least means that she's got *one* answer right today.

"Never mind," Lucy tells her, slipping her arm into Tally's. "At least if one of us fails, we'll all fail!"

"Yeah!" laughs Ayesha. "Miss Balogun said that Kingswood Academy will use these tests to figure out which set we're in for year seven. I guess we'll all be in bottom set together, then!"

Layla rolls her eyes. "Don't even talk about year seven," she says. "I don't want to think about it yet. We've still got plenty of time left before we have to leave – and there's the summer production still to come, don't forget."

"Your dance is *really* good," Tally tells Lucy as they make their way towards the playground.

Lucy flicks her hair back and smiles. "Thanks! Your lights are pretty good too."

"I still think you should have been Little Red," says Layla. "You'd have been amazing, Tally."

Tally can still remember the reaction she got when she said exactly the same thing on the day that Miss Balogun gave out the roles. It seems that it's OK for Layla to say it for her, but it isn't OK for her to say it about herself, which doesn't really make much sense. Not when it's the truth.

Although the truth doesn't seem to have much of a place when it comes to being the Tally they all seem to prefer.

She shakes her head. "I wouldn't have been as good as Carrie. She's the best person to play Little Red. I'm happy doing the lights."

The lie hurts, but the look of approval on the faces of her friends goes a little way towards easing the sting.

"I honestly didn't think you'd be so chill about it," Lucy says, squeezing Tally's arm. "I don't know what it is, but you're kind of easier to be around these days, Tally. No offence or anything."

Tally knows exactly what it is. She slips her hand into her pocket and runs the chain of the ladybird necklace through her fingers. It's true what Carrie's aunt told her. It *is* a lucky charm. And if it can help her get things right with her friends then it can definitely make sure that Dr Zennor's report says there is absolutely nothing wrong with her. She knows it can.

They reach the playground, and suddenly Carrie and her best friend Jasmine are right there in front of them, Jasmine's hands full of envelopes.

"It's my birthday in two weeks," she tells them. "And I'm having a party." She rifles through the envelopes and hands one to Lucy. "Here's an invitation for you," she says. "And one for you, Ayesha."

Tally takes a step away and stares into the distance. Jasmine is one of the most popular girls in their year and everyone wants to be her friend. She has a party every year, and most members of the class are given an invitation. Last year she had a pool party at the local leisure centre with huge inflatables, and the year before she had an amazing all-you-can-eat ice-cream party. It was all Layla could talk about for days afterwards, until Tally told her that if she heard one more thing about *sprinkles* or *chocolate sauce* or *hot fudge sundaes* then she'd never speak to Layla ever again.

Not that she even likes parties. The rules are always different, but nobody ever actually explains what they are, and Tally just spends the entire time trying to figure out what she's supposed to be doing or saying or thinking.

"I still haven't found my lucky necklace," says Carrie,

bringing Tally's attention back to now. "I've looked everywhere but it's completely disappeared."

"Do you think you could have dropped it somewhere?" asks Lucy, opening her envelope. "Ooh – a Zombie Laser Party? That sounds brilliant!"

Carrie frowns. "I just can't work out what happened to it. You all heard Miss Balogun ask the class if anyone took it and nobody said anything. I just really hate the idea that someone might have gone into my tray and stolen it."

"You don't need a lucky charm, though," says Jasmine. "You're amazing without it."

Carrie shakes her head. "I still want it back."

Jasmine gives her friend a sympathetic look and then returns to the business in hand. "I've been asking for a Zombie Laser party for years and my mum *finally* agreed. It's going to be *amazing*. Here's your invitation, Layla."

"Thanks!" Layla reaches out and grabs the envelope. "I've always wanted to do laser tag. Are you inviting the whole class? If you are, I'm definitely zapping Luke!"

She grins conspiratorially at Tally, who manages to give a weak smile in return.

"*Most* of the class," says Jasmine, grinning at Carrie. "All the cool people, anyway."

"What are you going to wear?" Lucy asks Ayesha and

Layla as the other two girls turn away. "I've got a new crop top that looks really good with my jeans."

"Definitely not a dress or a skirt," agrees Layla. "We need to be speedy if we're running around lasering zombies. You can't run fast in a skirt."

Tally clutches her fingers around the necklace. Maybe it doesn't work so well if it's hidden away inside her pocket? Maybe she needs to actually wear it so that the good luck can rub off on her?

"Oh, I almost forgot." Jasmine whirls around and faces Tally. "Here's your invitation. I hope you can come."

She holds out an envelope and when Tally looks down, she sees her name printed on the front. She swallows hard but doesn't move. What if it's a trick? She can count on the fingers of one hand the number of people who have ever invited her to a party and they're standing right here in front of her.

Jasmine and her legendary birthday celebrations is not one of them.

"Take it then," laughs Jasmine, thrusting it forward. "And you can be on my team. We need people who can run, and there's nobody as fast as you in the whole class! That's why I had to invite you – I definitely need to win on my own birthday!"

Tally releases the necklace and slowly accepts the invitation, turning it over in her hands as if she needs to check that it's real.

"Thank you," she says quietly. "I'd love to come to your party."

Jasmine links arms with Carrie, a strange smirk tugging at the corners of her mouth. It makes Tally feel uneasy and again, she wonders if this whole thing is some kind of prank.

"I told you that she'd say yes," Carrie says quietly, smiling at Tally. "Jasmine wasn't sure if you'd want to come or not, but I told her that everyone loves a good party."

Tally gulps. She's only been invited because of Carrie.

"Wait!" Tally steps nearer to her. "About your necklace…"

"Yes?" The other girl spins round and regards Tally with serious eyes.

Tally swallows hard. "I'm sure nobody took it from your tray. That would be really bad. You must have dropped it somewhere."

Carrie scrunches up her nose. "You're probably right. Maybe it'll turn up."

Then both girls are gone, and Tally is pulled into a long and animated conversation about Zombie laser tag and whether there will be a prize for the person with the highest score and maybe pizza afterwards because Jasmine's parties always have the *best* food.

But all Tally can think about is that now, after all this time, she finally knows what it feels like to be lucky. And she doesn't want to be ungrateful or anything, and she *thinks* she's pleased that she's been invited to the party because even though she hates parties (and this one sounds worse than most), it's nice to be included – but actually, being lucky doesn't feel quite as great as she thought it would.

CHAPTER 17

"OK, year six." Miss Balogun puts her book down on her desk and looks at the class. "You've done really well this morning and you've all earned yourselves a nice lunch break."

She walks across the room to peer out of the window, and Tally puts her hand in her pocket to rub the ladybird necklace between her fingers. But not even the lucky charm can stop Miss Balogun's next words – words that Tally dreads to hear.

"It's still raining so it'll be wet play," she announces. "Once you've had your lunch, you can come back up here and get the wet play boxes from the cupboard." She picks up her bag and gives them all a stern look. "And if I hear any reports of people being daft, then it'll be five minutes removed from Friday afternoon's

Golden Time – is that understood?"

The class murmur their assent and everyone packs away their pencil cases and books before heading off to the hall, eagerly discussing what games they can play once they've finished eating. Tally dawdles behind, and, once she's sitting at the year six lunch table, eats her cheese sandwich as slowly as possible. Wet lunchtime is the absolute worst thing that can happen at school, and she's in no hurry to get back to the classroom.

But she can't hide out in the hall for ever. The sound hits her ears when she's only halfway up the stairs, and by the time she steps inside the classroom it's almost unbearable. She doesn't know how everyone else can just sit there while the noise crashes and roils all around them like furious waves breaking on the shore, but nobody seems to mind. She picks her way between the desks to where Layla is playing a frantic card game with Lucy and Ayesha, and sits down beside them, trying to breathe deeply in an effort to stop them from seeing how much she hates this.

"Snap!" screeches Lucy, slamming her hand on to the table.

Tally flinches but nobody notices.

"Deal Tally into the next round," demands Layla, pushing all the cards towards Lucy. "Let's play again."

Lucy starts to shuffle the deck and Tally glances around the room. Over in the corner, Luke and Ameet are playing a very loud game of table football, and next to them a group of kids are stacking wooden blocks into a tall tower. As Tally watches, the blocks wobble and teeter and then crash to the ground.

Everyone laughs.

Tally wraps her arms around her stomach and tries to breathe slowly.

"I'll go first because I won the last round," announces Lucy, slapping a card down in front of them. "Your turn, Ayesha."

A movement by the door gets Tally's attention. She looks over and sees Miles standing very still, as if he's debating whether to enter the room or not. A sudden shout from the direction of the table football makes him frown, and then suddenly Mrs Bernard is there, bending down to say something into Miles's ear. He nods and smiles and then he's gone, away from the chaos and heading down the stairs.

Mrs Bernard looks like she's about to follow him, but at the last minute she pauses and looks right at Tally.

"*Koala Club*?" she mouths, giving Tally a thumbs-up sign before turning and walking after Miles.

And Tally wants nothing more than to get up and leave the room. The idea of spending the rest of lunchtime in the library, snuggled up into a chair and reading a book in the peace and quiet, makes her whole body feel warm. She's finished the world records book that Miles lent her, but he's told her that there's an entire shelf of them in the library and promised to find her a good one to read next. She could go down there and hang out with him and Mrs Bernard and escape the bedlam of the classroom. She pushes back her chair and starts to rise, but then a voice booms out above all the other noise.

"Where did *Weirdo Edwards* go?" Luke looms over their table, his eyes glinting the way they always do when he's about to say something awful. "Did you see his face when he was standing in the doorway? I thought he was about to *cry*!"

"Go away, Luke," says Ayesha. "And don't be mean about Miles. You know he's a bit different."

"You can say that again." Luke smirks at Ameet, who has come to stand beside him. "Although isn't Miss Balogun always telling us to *mix up our vocabulary*? I think we should use some better words to describe him. Like *peculiar*."

"Or *odd*," adds Ameet. "Or *strange*."

"He *is* a bit strange," agrees Luke. "You know he's not got any friends? He spends all his time in the library."

"I'm sure he's got friends." Layla sounds cross. "Don't be so unkind."

"Oh yeah, sure." Luke looks at her. "I forgot about all his *pretend* friends. He's got the World's Strongest Man and the World's Fastest Woman and the World's Oldest Person. And don't forget the World's Smallest Dog and the World's Biggest Teddy Bear. He loves hanging out with that teddy bear – they're best mates." He sighs deeply, as if Miles's behaviour causes him pain. "I know the best way to describe him. He's *the World's Freakiest Kid*."

Lucy giggles, and when Tally looks around, even Layla has a slight smile pulling at the edges of her mouth. She sinks back into her seat and clenches her fists under the table. This isn't fair. She should tell Luke that he's wrong and that Miles *does* have a friend.

She should stand up and defend him.

Luke makes a clicking sound with his tongue and shakes his head. "Let's face it. He's *Weirdo Edwards*, and nothing any of you can say will ever change that. He's always clutching that weird old book like it's the most important thing in the world to him. He's odd and that's a fact."

He glances at Tally and jerks his head in a quick nod, as if daring her to speak out against him. And then he walks away. And Tally lets him. She picks up the cards in front of her, and she starts to play the game, letting the noise of the classroom drown out the screams in her head that are telling her she's doing the wrong thing. She doesn't get up and call out Luke for being an atrocious human being. She doesn't let her feet do what they are begging her to do – take her out of here and straight to the sanctuary of the library.

Because for the first time in ages, Luke didn't say anything horrible about *her*. Which means that she is winning. And it is an undisputable truth that when Luke is calling Miles *Weirdo Edwards*, he isn't calling her *Weirdo Adams*. When Luke is being mean to Miles, the spotlight is off her and she can blend into the background, like the chameleon that it is safest for her to be.

And maybe she should have spoken up for Miles, but if she'd done that, then everyone would wonder why. Maybe they would think that she's just like him, but she isn't – not in any single way. There's nothing wrong with her, no matter what Dr Zennor writes in her stupid report – not the way that there is with Miles. He doesn't hide how he's feeling and Tally doesn't know if that's because he *can't* or he *won't* but, either way, Miles doesn't pretend. He is just *him*.

And people are just mean.

All Tally has to do is hide her differences. Otherwise it'll be *her* being called *peculiar* and *odd* and *strange*.

It'll be her being called the *freak*.

After lunch, Miss Balogun calls everyone to be quiet.

"I have some sad news," she says, her face looking solemn. "You all know that Carrie wasn't here yesterday, and today I've had a phone call from her mother. Carrie's got a rather horrid virus and her mum is fairly sure that she won't be back at school for the next few weeks."

She pauses and as the news sinks in, the classroom erupts in a burst of chatter.

"But it's the summer production in two weeks!" yells Lucy. "What are we going to do?"

Miss Balogun holds her hand up in the air and waits for the noise to die down.

"I'm not sure," she tells them. "It's very short notice to get someone else to learn the part of Little Red, but I suppose whoever does it could hold the script while they're on stage."

Tally pulls the necklace out of her pocket and keeps it

hidden in her hand, pressing it tightly inside her clenched fist. She wants to stand up and tell Miss Balogun that she could do it. She wants to shout out that she's here and she's ready, but she's learnt enough over the last few months to know that people don't like it when you say you're good at something. You get told that you're bragging or *up yourself*, and it doesn't even matter if you're genuinely the best, you still have to pretend that you aren't.

But if only she could raise her hand and tell everyone that—

"Tally knows all the words!" calls Layla, suddenly. She jumps to her feet and beams at Miss Balogun. "She's been learning them for ages and she'd be amazing at playing Little Red!"

Miss Balogun stares at Tally, who feels her cheeks start to flush.

"Tally?" asks the teacher. "Is this true? Do you know Little Red's lines?"

Tally gulps. "Yes," she whispers.

"And she can sing too!" announces Layla. "I've heard her."

"Me too!" declares Lucy.

"And me!" Ayesha raises her hand. "She's brilliant!"

Tally isn't sure why neither Lucy nor Ayesha have ever

complimented her on her singing voice before if they think she's that good, but now isn't the time to question it. All around her, kids are nodding and grinning and saying how great she'll be, and for a brief moment she wonders if she's fallen asleep at her desk and is having the best dream she's ever had in her life.

Miss Balogun claps her hands for order.

"Well then," she says, smiling at Tally. "I think the show can still go on! If you're happy to step in and save the day, Tally?"

On the outside, Tally is nodding and smiling and agreeing that she will play the part of Little Red, although it's really very sad that Carrie won't be here. On the inside she is bubbling over with excitement and delight. Now she won't have to tell Mum and Dad that she's only in charge of the lights. Now she'll get to show everyone just what she is capable of doing. Now it's finally going to be her time to shine and everyone can forget all about Dr Zennor and any thoughts that she might be *different*.

In her hand, the lucky charm feels hot. She slips it back into her pocket where it will be safe. It didn't give much luck to Carrie, that's for sure – but it's certainly helping her catch a break.

Everything is going to be just *perfect*.

CHAPTER 18

Tally sees the postman walking up the garden path. She races out of her room and down the stairs just as he pushes the envelopes through the letterbox. She's been doing this for *days* – ever since she overheard Mum telling Dad that the report from Dr Zennor was due any time now. She scoops the post off the floor and rifles through.

A flyer for the local swimming pool.

A bill addressed to Mr K Adams.

A postcard for Nell.

No report from the doctor.

Tally isn't entirely sure what she's going to do with the report when it does arrive. It won't be addressed to *her*, she knows that – even though it's *her* head and *her* body and *her* life, nobody will think that she deserves to be the first person to find out what the doctor thinks about her.

And it's really wrong to open post that isn't addressed to you, maybe even a criminal offence.

But it's about *her*.

And she can't just wait until all the adults decide that she should be told whatever it is that they think they know. That's not right. But the post has arrived now and there's definitely no report so she's safe, at least for today.

She's still feeling safe when Mum calls her into the kitchen partway through the afternoon and asks her to sit down at the table. The safe feeling lasts as Dad walks in and sits down opposite her, a big, awkward smile on his face. But the safe feeling starts to wobble when Mum brings her a cup of hot chocolate and sits down next to her with the same smile as Dad.

"I'm missing my programme," Tally says. "Can I go?"

"In a minute," Mum tells her. "Dad and I want to talk to you first." She glances at Dad, as if she isn't sure what to say next, and now Tally really wants to leave.

"You know how you're amazing at making music, but Nell finds it hard to sing in tune?" says Dad, completely randomly.

"And how Nell enjoys trying new kinds of food, but you aren't so keen on eating different things?" adds Mum, leaping onto the conversation. "It's what makes us all unique and special – we all have things that we're good at and things that we find more of a struggle."

Tally stares at the table. She does not like where this is going.

"Well, we want to have a chat with you about the things that you find tricky and the things that you're great at doing." Dad leans forward and smiles at Tally. "And talk about why some things might be a bit more difficult for you."

"Did you manage to print it all out?" Mum asks Dad. "The printer was playing up yesterday."

Dad nods and pushes a stack of paper forward. Tally cranes to read the top page and sees her name and date of birth. A prickling sensation crawls up her legs and she starts to tap her foot.

"Do you remember the appointment that you had with Dr Zennor?" asks Mum.

If she weren't so scared, Tally would laugh. Do they honestly think that she might have forgotten about the fact that all these weeks have been about waiting; waiting to find out whether she's good enough or not?

"Well, we've had the report back and we want to share it with you," Mum continues.

No. That can't be true. She's been checking the post

and there's been no sign of a report. This is exactly what she *didn't* want to happen – an ambush by Mum and Dad when they know *everything* and she knows *nothing*. Tally's stomach flips over and she blinks hard, trying to keep the tears away.

"It's all fine," says Dad in a hurry, catching sight of Tally's face. "Nothing to be worried about."

"Nothing at all!" Mum's voice is rushed and high-pitched.

Tally's shoulders slump in relief. It's going to be OK. There's nothing to worry about. She's normal and good and everything can go back to how it used to be.

"So can I go now?" She pushes her chair back and starts to stand up.

"Just wait a moment." Mum puts her hand on Tally's arm. "It's important that we help you understand what this means."

"Understand what *what* means?" Tally sinks back into her seat. "You said that there was nothing to worry about."

"And there isn't." Mum takes hold of Tally's hand and strokes it gently, the way she usually likes. "Your brain is wired a little differently to most other kids, but that's what gives us all the great bits of you as well as the things you find hard. It's what makes you *you*."

Tally raises her eyes to stare at Mum. "What do you mean? What's wrong with my brain?"

"There's nothing *wrong*," says Dad. "That's not it at all. Look – it's a bit like this." He gets up and comes to crouch down beside her chair. "People's brains operate in different ways. Like, most kids have an Xbox for their brain, but you have a PlayStation. So some games that work on an Xbox aren't compatible with a PlayStation and vice versa. Everybody has challenges, and we're lucky that we know what yours is called."

Tally clamps her hands over her ears and starts to hum as loudly as she can. She doesn't know what he's on about with all this stupid talk about her being a PlayStation, but she does know that she doesn't want to hear anything else.

"Tally." Mum gently pulls her hands away from her ears and holds them in between her own. "We need you to listen to this. The doctors all agree that you are autistic, which is something that we already thought might be true, isn't it?"

And there it is.

The word.

Tally stops humming and focuses on the warmth of Mum's hands.

"Autism is probably the reason why you don't like

wearing certain clothes or eating certain food, and it's why, sometimes, your brain gets overwhelmed with everything that you're feeling," explains Mum. "And it's also the reason why you're so caring to animals and brilliantly funny and super imaginative."

"Autism isn't an illness or a disease." Dad gazes up at Tally. "It's different but it's definitely not *wrong*."

Tally wrenches her hands away from Mum and clenches them into two fists.

"If it isn't wrong then why did you tell me?" she growls. "Why did you want to find out in the first place?"

"Because now that we know, we can help to make things easier for you." Mum smiles at Tally. "And knowing is *good*, Tally. We all need to know who we are, otherwise how can we make sense of ourselves?"

"Great." Tally shoves her chair back and stands abruptly, nearly causing Dad to topple on to the floor. He steadies himself with his hand and pushes himself up to standing, and Tally knows that he's about to try and give her a hug.

"Don't," she warns him. "Just don't."

Dad hesitates and then goes back to sit on his side of the table. Tally glowers down at both of them, her face screwed up with rage.

"Nobody asked me if I wanted to know, did they?" she

spits. "I did everything you all asked of me and I was on my best behaviour for that stupid appointment with Dr Zennor, and this is what I get in return? Being told that I'm autistic?"

"It isn't a punishment, sweetheart." Mum's voice is quiet but firm. "Being autistic means that you're different, not less."

"But I don't want to be different!" howls Tally, letting everything go. "What's the point in me trying so hard, every single day, to be the same as everyone else if you're just going to tell me that I'm *different* and there's nothing that I can do about it?"

"That *is* the point," Dad tells her. "We don't want you to have to work so hard. You're our incredible, wonderful girl and we want you to be able to be yourself."

Tally's eyes flicker from side to side, gazing at the room that up to a few minutes ago was as familiar as her own hand. Not any longer. Everything has a slight sheen over the top now, as if she's looking at it through a filter on her phone.

"You can't tell anyone else." The thought whips into her head and bounces around her brain, fizzing and spluttering with terror. "I mean it. I don't want anyone else to know."

Mum shoots a quick look at Dad. It's fast but Tally is faster. She sees everything and she knows exactly what that look means.

"Who have you told?" Her hands have started flapping at her sides and she folds them across her body, tucking them under each armpit to hold them down. "Who knows?"

"Tally," starts Mum. "It's really important that people understand who you are so that they can help you when things are tough."

Tally steps back but her eyes don't leave Mum's.

"Who. Have. You. Told?"

Dad speaks up. "We've mentioned it to Auntie Tish," he says calmly, as if his words aren't stabbing into Tally's heart with every syllable. "And Nell knows. We wanted to explain it to her so that she'd be able to understand when you're finding things tough."

"Who else." Tally is still staring at Mum. "I know there's someone else."

Mum closes her eyes briefly, as if this isn't how she imagined this conversation going. When she opens them, Tally can see that she was right. If it was written across her face in permanent marker pen, it couldn't be any clearer.

"I've spoken to Miss Balogun," she says quietly. "One of the reasons for trying to get a diagnosis is to help you at school, and we can't do that if nobody knows. I'm sorry if you think we should have told you first. Maybe you're right – but this is new for us too, you know?"

Dad gives a little chuckle. "We're all going to be learning about the right way to handle this together," he says. "And I guess we're going to make a few mistakes along the way."

Tally pushes her jaw together so hard that she can feel her back teeth starting to grind. They are *not* all going to be doing this together. Nobody has flung a word at Mum and Dad and told them that this is who they are now. And when *they* make a mistake, they're allowed to get over it. She's never going to be allowed to get over this, is she?

"It's a lot to take in, we know that." Mum's face is a bit red, as if she's been out in the sun for too long. "But we can keep talking about it, and we're right here if you have any questions, OK?"

Dad walks across to the counter where the biscuit tin is kept.

"And if we don't know the answers to your questions then we'll find out," he says, unscrewing the lid and walking back to where Tally is standing. "But this changes nothing, OK? You're still our fierce, hilarious kid, and we're still your annoying-yet-brilliant parents."

He offers her the tin, but Tally shakes her head. Nell was wrong. A biscuit can't make everything better.

"You'd better not tell anyone else," she warns them, narrowing her eyes. "I mean it. I'll never forgive you if you do."

Mum and Dad nod in agreement, and after flinging them one final glare, Tally stalks out of the kitchen and up to her bedroom.

It's her life and she should be the one who gets to choose who knows about this. And she chooses nobody.

Nobody at school can ever find out.

Not ever.

Dear Taylor Swift,

I am writing to you because a) I know that you will understand and b) I don't have anyone else to talk to. I know you are world-famous and may not read this, but I know you are really good with your fans, so here's hoping! Something big has happened and I don't know how I'm supposed to be feeling about it. Mum and Dad are acting like everything is going to be fine now, but nothing has changed, has it? I'm still me. I'm still different.

That's what Mum said anyway, when she was trying to tell me that being autistic doesn't make me worse than anyone else. She thought that she was helping, but being told I'm different is the worst thing I can hear. It's patronizing. Like, they're basically trying to come up with a nicer sounding way of telling me I AM worse than others. It makes me feel absolutely rubbish. Who wants to be "different"? Not me, for sure – I just want to fit in and be the same as everyone else. I'm fed up of feeling like the rotten pear in the fruit bowl that everyone avoids. It's not a nice feeling. It makes me feel like I'm contaminated with something awful that nobody else wants to catch.

Having to talk to the doctor and share the parts of myself that I keep secret was so embarrassing. I actually thought I'd done quite a good job of keeping the real me hidden, but obviously not. Although I must admit the experience wasn't as bad as I had imagined it would be. I had pictured the doctor peering into my face, asking things like, "What is the most violent thing you have done to your parents?" But those kinds of questions never got asked. Not to me anyway.

And now we all have the answer to the perpetual problem that is me – I have Autistic Spectrum Disorder with traits of Pathological Demand Avoidance, which you probably think is a fancy way of saying that I don't like being told what to do. Actually, that's not true at all. It's more that being told what to do makes my heart beat faster and my legs feel tingly, like I need to run away. Basically, being told what to do makes me feel scared.

Who wants to be that person? I feel like I've been crushed under something really heavy. I want to be Tally Adams, star of stage and screen. Tally Adams, champion horse-rider. Or even Tally Adams, totally normal kid.

I don't want to be Tally Adams, autistic person.

So guess what, Taylor Swift? I have a solution. They can take away their stupid diagnosis. I don't want it and I'm not going to be it.

Love Tally Adams,
Your number one fan

CHAPTER 19

"And that's it for today," calls Miss Balogun, clapping her hands. "Well done, everyone, for a wonderful rehearsal and especially you, Tally! That was brilliant! I can't believe how word-perfect you are already. What a star you are!"

Tally smiles.

Word-perfect. That's what Miss Balogun just said, and it's the absolute best way to describe how Tally feels right now. Nobody is calling her *weirdo* or *different* or *difficult.* She is *brilliant* and *wonderful* and a *star.*

She is word-perfect and she has every intention of staying that way. She just has to make sure that nobody finds out about the whole autism thing, which shouldn't be too hard. She just has to keep on making sure that she does what everyone else does.

"I knew you'd be an amazing Little Red," says Layla

as they pack away the benches. "You're so good, Tally."

"Not as good as Carrie, though." The whisper comes from nowhere, and when Tally spins round, she can't tell who said it.

"I'm so excited for the performance," continues Layla, as if she hasn't heard anything. "And we've got Jasmine's laser party tomorrow afternoon too! I can't wait!"

Tally grins back at her. "I know! The party is going to be great."

"And you're both going to wear your crop tops like we all agreed, yeah?" Lucy and Ayesha have come up behind them. "We're going to look excellent!"

"Definitely!" says Layla.

"Definitely," echoes Tally.

"Definitely *not*," states Mum, her hands on her hips. "You're not wearing that to the party, Tally. Go back upstairs and get changed into something more suitable."

Tally scowls at Mum. "But I want to wear *this*."

Mum scowls back. "No."

"Why not?" Tally straightens her shoulders and stands up as tall as she possibly can. "What's wrong with it? Don't you think I look nice?"

"You look great, sweetheart," says Dad, choosing this moment to walk into the kitchen.

"Kevin!" snaps Mum. "You're not helping."

Dad looks between the two of them, his face wrinkled in confusion. "What have I done wrong now? I said that she looks great."

"And I'm saying that this top, while perfectly fine to be worn in the garden, is not appropriate for a laser tag party," says Mum, pushing the words out between her gritted teeth.

"Oh." Dad looks at Tally again. "Yes. I can see that."

Tally frowns at them both. "What was the point in buying it for me if you weren't going to let me wear it?"

Mum sighs. "If I remember correctly, you begged and begged for this crop top, and I finally gave in and bought it for you under the strict understanding that it wasn't to be worn in public."

"That does seem like a bit of a daft purchase…" mumbles Dad before registering that Mum is giving him one of her death stares.

"Have *you* ever been clothes shopping with her?" Mum's eyebrows are so high that they have almost disappeared into her hairline. "It's like an SAS endurance event. I end up buying her something just to stop the torture."

"So can I wear it?" risks Tally. "We need to leave now or I'm going to be late."

"Then you'd better hurry yourself up those stairs and put on something decent," says Mum. "I've put your favourite T-shirt out on your bed – it'll be perfect for all that running around."

"I promised the others that I'd wear it." Tally tries a new tactic. "They're all wearing crop tops and I'm going to look totally different to them if I don't wear mine. You don't want me to be different, do you?"

Mum's face softens and Tally relaxes her shoulders. Mum knows how important this party is to her – there's no way that she'll make her stand out by forcing her to wear the stupid T-shirt. Not when they've been trying really hard not to upset her since that awful conversation about the diagnosis.

"They won't be wearing crop tops," Mum says, putting her hand on Tally's arm. "Not if their mothers have any sense. Now go and get changed and we can get you there on time. I know you hate being late."

It is hard for Tally to describe the feeling that is currently pulsing through her body. All she knows is that something bad – very bad – is about to happen, and she is powerless to stop it. It feels like standing on a train track and watching a train hurtling towards her and feeling desperate to run away only her legs are frozen and so all she can do is watch.

She swallows hard and forces her feet to move. She doesn't even want to go to the party any more, not now that Mum has ruined it, but she hasn't got a choice. She has to go upstairs and put on the T-shirt and then walk outside to the car, where she has to listen to Mum telling her that she's going to have such a fun time, and isn't it lovely of Jasmine to have invited her, and the whole time she is fighting the urge to curl up into a tiny ball and make herself invisible so that the bad thing can't find her.

"Here we are!" trills Mum as they pull up outside a long, squat building. "We're only a few minutes late. Shall I come in with you?"

Tally shakes her head and makes her hand reach for the door handle of the car.

"No."

"Well, have a lovely time." Mum suddenly looks concerned. "I really don't mind walking in with you and saying hello to Jasmine's mum."

"I'm fine on my own," growls Tally. "I don't need you to come in with me. I'm not a baby."

And then she's out of the car and walking towards the

entrance. She *isn't* fine on her own and she really, *really* wants Mum to jump out and walk into the party with her. But sometimes, when she's scared, she says things that she doesn't mean. And sometimes – the worst times – Mum believes her.

"Tally! You're here!" Layla hurtles up to the doorway where Tally is standing. "Come on, they're just about to give out the laser guns."

She drags Tally towards the far side of the room, where almost all of the year six class is standing and listening to a man explaining the safety details. Tally glances around, seeing that virtually everyone is here. In fact, the only people missing are Carrie, who is still unwell, and Miles who was presumably not invited. Tally shudders, like a spider has just crawled up her spine. She can only hope that Miles has been so engrossed in his world records books that he didn't even know there *was* a party.

"You didn't wear the top," hisses Lucy as they stand next to her and Ayesha. "We all agreed."

Layla shrugs. "My mum wouldn't let me," she whispers. "She said that I'm ten years old and going to a laser party, not eighteen and going out clubbing."

"Mine too," adds Tally, only now noticing that Layla is clad in a sensible T-shirt, just like she is.

Lucy tosses her hair over her shoulder and pulls a face. "Lucky for me and Ayesha that our mums are cool, then."

Tally frowns. The idea of whether her mum is cool or uncool isn't something that she's ever given a lot of time to thinking about.

She's just a mum. That's it.

"So, let's recap. You need to be careful when you're handling a weapon," says the man at the front as some other members of staff start to hand out the laser guns. "They've got a bit of weight to them and could give someone a nasty bump on the head if you go swinging them around. The aim of the game is to hide from each other in the obstacle arena and take tactical shots, not dash around like headless chickens, OK? So no running, and take it steady."

"You're never going to catch me!" screams Ameet, sprinting towards the arena.

"Last one in position is a zombie loser!" yells Ayesha, leaping after him. "Let's *do* this!"

"I said *no running*," shouts the safety man before shaking his head at Jasmine's mum who is standing nearby. "Every damn time I tell them, and do they ever listen? No, they do not. I don't know why I waste my breath…"

Tally takes her gun and walks slowly towards the arena.

"Excellent!" calls the safety man. "Finally, someone sensible who is doing what I've asked. Thank you!"

Tally ignores him and keeps walking. She isn't being slow because he's asked her to be. She's being slow because what lies on the other side of the barrier is unknown and scary and she suddenly wishes, with all of her heart, that she was back at home with Mum, Dad and Nell. Bored and left out, but safe.

Taking a deep breath, she pushes through the gate that leads to the obstacle arena.

"Take up your positions!" yells the safety man. "And remember what I said – I want a nice, clean game. Anyone with any issues needs to report to me at the equipment station. Now let's release the zombies!"

And the world turns upside-down.

It's a triple threat. The main lights go out and are replaced with flickering, strobing, manic lights that sweep across the arena. At the same time, the whole place is flooded with a thudding, pounding beat that Tally can feel under her feet. And as she stands there, trying not to let the panic overwhelm her, she feels people rushing past her, knocking her arms and shoulders as they race to hide from the zombies.

"Get out of the way!" yells Luke, shoving her so hard

that she stumbles and almost falls to the ground. "You can't just stand there."

He's absolutely right. She can't just stand there. She thought that playing *Infection* in the playground was bad enough, but this is fifty times worse. She needs to get out of here and find Jasmine's mum and tell her that she wants to go home.

"Tally!" It's Layla, red in the face and panting for breath. "Are you all right?"

She could tell her. Layla is her best friend and she'll understand. She'll help Tally to leave the arena and get to safety. She should tell her.

"...I'm fine."

Even as she says the words, Tally's brain is screaming at her for being so weak. She isn't fine in the slightest, she knows that. But she'll be even less fine if she gives up now. If she walks away and asks to go home, then everything she's worked for so far will be for nothing. Everyone else is having a wonderful time, and she doesn't know why she isn't too, but she does know that if she lets them see how she's feeling then she'll be back to being on the outside in two seconds flat. And that's *not* how it's supposed to be now. Not now that she's finally achieved her goal and is accepted as one of them.

"Shall we go and hide out in the ball pit?" yells Layla. "If we sink down really low we can lie in wait for anyone that comes along and they won't even see us until it's too late!"

Tally nods and follows behind as Layla leads her deeper into the arena. With any luck the ball pit will be really deep and she'll be able to sink to the bottom and stay there until this whole, terrible ordeal is over. She has to do whatever it takes to show them all that she's just the same as they are, even if that stupid report from Dr Zennor says that she isn't and Mum and Dad keep looking at her as if they've got a gazillion things on their mind. The last thing she needs is for Jasmine's mum to ring them and say that she can't cope with something as *easy* as a party.

Otherwise she'll be no better off than Miles.

CHAPTER 20

The tiger stares out of the bedroom window at the world beyond the glass. The sun is shining brightly, making the garden look warm and inviting, but the tiger cannot go outside. All the tiger can do is press her nose to the window and watch the other animals as they go about their daily lives, making it look so, so easy. The tiger isn't sure about very much right now, but one thing she does know is that they must all be faking it. There is nothing easy about getting up and getting dressed and having to listen and talk and say the right things. There is nothing easy about being told what you should be doing or where you should be going or how you should be thinking – even if everyone else does act like it's no big deal.

The tiger has done everything she can to make it easier for herself, in her fight to be accepted as one of them. She has observed the other animals and tried to copy what they do. She has squished herself into shapes that should have been impossible – and do you know how hard it is for a tiger to pass as an alligator or a giraffe or a hippopotamus? All she ever wanted was to be like everyone else and to fit in.

And she's *done it*. She's got the lead role in the production and she was invited to the party. Nobody is calling her unkind names, and yesterday Jasmine told her that her acting is amazing. If someone had told her two months ago that these things were going to happen, she'd have hardly been able to believe it. She's got everything she ever wanted.

She is the luckiest tiger in the world.

Even if she doesn't really feel like a tiger any more.

Even if, actually, she isn't really sure who she is. And the one thing she *does* know about herself is something that she can't even bear to think about, never mind share with anyone else.

"Can we have quiet, please?" calls Miss Balogun.

Tally stands on the dark stage, waiting for her cue. She can sense everyone else nearby, but nobody is making a sound. It's peaceful and calm, and for a second Tally can breathe properly.

And then the lights come on and the music starts and she steps forward. She can do this. She's good at pretending to be someone else. In fact, pretending to be someone else is a lot easier than trying to figure out who she's supposed to be. She can hang out with the popular kids playing the part of "regular girl" and she can sit in class and play the part of "quiet kid" and all she has to do is follow the others. Not that she has to mimic anyone when it comes to playing the part of Little Red, though. No matter how often people try to tell her how Carrie played the role, Tally knows that she can make it her own. She knows that acting is where she truly shines, and she doesn't have to copy anyone else.

After the rehearsal, Miles beckons her across to where he's standing at the light and sound desk. Miss Balogun is leading everyone out of the hall and back to class, and Tally hesitates as she watches Layla leave. She's barely spoken to Miles since she got the part of Little Red – there hasn't been time in between all the rehearsing and then hanging out with the other kids. She's told herself that she's just been really busy, but she knows that isn't the whole truth.

She's worked really hard to earn her place with the

others, and she doesn't want to do anything to jeopardize it. But that isn't the whole truth either.

The whole truth is never just one thing. The whole truth is always made up of lots of smaller things that weave and flow around each other, and more than one thing can be true at the same time.

Tally *has* been busy. And she *doesn't* want anything to mess up her newfound popular status, not after wanting it for so long. But neither of those truths are the entire reason for the fact that she has been ignoring Miles. One, tiny, little truth is missing, and even though Tally has tried very hard to keep it squashed deep down inside, it swirls and flurries its way up, up, up until she can't pretend any longer.

The report from Dr Zennor. The autism diagnosis. They've given her the same word as Miles, but when Tally looks at Miles she doesn't see herself, not even a little bit. And she can't risk anyone else seeing him when they look at her. So she's trying to stay away.

Tally starts to turn. But then Miles waves at her again, and she can't just ignore him. She was ignored all the time before she got the part of Little Red, and she knows how awful it is. She only has to stay for a minute, she tells herself as she walks across to the lighting desk, and nobody is even here to see. She'll talk to him for a moment and then she can go and find Layla and the rest of them outside and listen while everyone tells her what a brilliant actor she is.

"You weren't standing in the right position for the spotlight," Miles tells her, making frantic notes on his plan.

"Yes I was." Tally glares at him. She came over here to be nice, not to be insulted. "I was standing exactly where I was supposed to be."

"You weren't." Miles shakes his head and thrusts his piece of paper in front of her. "Look. Carrie always stands *here*." He points to a dot on the page. "But you were standing *here*." He stabs at the plan with a red pen. "You were at least twenty centimetres to the left."

"So what?" Tally can feel her frustration starting to build. "Twenty centimetres is nothing."

"It's *everything*," says Miles, his voice sounding shocked. "But more importantly, it isn't where Carrie always stands."

Tally shrugs. "It's where Carrie *used* to stand," she tells him. "I'm not Carrie and I'll stand where I like."

Miles slowly raises his eyes from the plan and looks right at Tally. It's the first time he's ever looked properly at her face, and she can tell that he's feeling awkward, but that doesn't stop her from glaring at him. It's bad enough that other people keep *helpfully* telling her how Carrie played the part of Little Red – she doesn't need Miles joining in too.

"But you'll ruin the whole lighting plan," Miles whispers. "I set it all up for Carrie, and you have to stand in the right place or everything will be wrong."

Tally can see the panic in his eyes and her heart suddenly feels heavy. She opens her mouth to reassure him, and then the sound of feet makes her hesitate.

"What's going on?"

Tally turns to see Lucy, Ayesha, Luke and Ameet closing in behind her.

"Why are you talking to *him*?" asks Luke, jerking his head at Miles. "It's break-time now."

"I wasn't," Tally says quickly. "Let's go."

"What did you think about Jasmine's party at the weekend? It was wild, wasn't it?"

Tally starts to speak and then stops. The question isn't directed at her.

"Oh, sorry!" Luke slaps his hand to his mouth in fake shock and stares right at Miles. "You weren't invited, were you? My bad – it's just that everyone else was there, so I forgot that Jasmine didn't actually want you to come. On account of you being such a weirdo loser and everything."

Miles puts his lighting plan down on the table and starts making hurried marks on the page, his glasses slipping down his nose, the way that they always do when he's trying to concentrate.

"Go away, Luke." The words come out before Tally can stop them.

Lucy makes a gasping sound, and Tally doesn't have to look at Luke's face to see that she's just made the biggest mistake of her life.

"Are you standing up for Weirdo Edwards?" Luke's voice is slithering and slimy. "Are you actually friends with him or something?"

Ameet snorts with laughter.

"I thought you liked hanging out with all of us?" demands Luke, his eyes glittering. "Well, you have to choose. Us or the freak boy?"

And suddenly everything is very still. Tally holds her breath and watches as some part of her that she can't quite control weighs up her options. It's as if she is standing at a crossroads and is being forced to choose which path to take. Her fizzing head and angry hands want her to go one way, her fingers curling themselves into a fist, ready to slam hard into Luke's smug face without a single care for the consequences. Her thudding heart and swirling stomach want her to go the other way, pleading with her to run away as fast as she can and find some space where she can try to figure out how to retain some of the status she has fought so hard to win.

But the tiger, who is rearing up inside her, is telling her something entirely different. It's telling her that right now, in this moment, she is making a bigger choice than whether to go left or right; to run or to fight; to choose acceptance or isolation. An even bigger choice than deciding whether to be friends with Miles or everyone else. It's telling her that while all of that matters, none of it is as important as choosing who *she* is.

A quiet, tiny voice is whispering in her head that if she keeps trying to reinvent herself as someone else and she *still* doesn't fit in, then maybe it's about time to stop trying to be who they want her to be and start being *her*. That if every new Tally she shows them is wrong, then she might as well accept being the one, true Tally. And that her liking her real self is maybe, just maybe, more important than other people liking who they *think* she is.

"Miles is my friend." Her voice is strong and clear, which she's glad about because she's fairly sure that her legs are shaking. "Leave him alone. You can't just go around being nasty to people all the time."

"Yeah, leave us alone," mumbles Miles, pushing his glasses back up his nose. "Just go away."

Luke smirks. "What was that, Weirdo Edwards? Did you have something to say? Say it again – to my face this time."

He lurches towards Miles but the tiger is quicker. She lunges forward, putting herself between the two boys.

"Get lost, Luke," she hisses. "If you lay one finger on him, then I'm going to scream so loudly that Miss Balogun is going to be back down here in two seconds flat, and then I'm going to tell her all about you and the things you say about other people, and I'm pretty sure that she'll phone up your dad and he'll have to come into school and you'll have to explain why you're such an ignorant, despicable pig."

Luke hesitates. "What makes you think that she'll believe you over me? I'll just tell her that you're making the whole thing up."

"Because I'll tell her too." Miles steps out from behind Tally.

"And me," adds Ayesha. "You've gone too far this time, Luke." She turns to Lucy. "You'll back Tally up, won't you?"

Lucy glances quickly between Tally and Luke and then nods. "Yeah, of course I will."

Luke glares at Lucy and Ayesha before turning his gaze on to Tally.

"You're going to be sorry that you messed with me," he tells her quietly. "I see you, Weirdo Adams. And I'm going to make sure that everyone else sees you too."

Tally plants her feet firmly apart and speaks with a confidence that, while new and a little bit shaky, feels rooted deep down inside of her. "Go ahead. I'm not scared of you, Luke."

Luke gives a little laugh. "How perfect is that? Weirdo Adams and Weirdo Edwards. Best friends for ever."

"Call him that one more time," warns Tally, narrowing her eyes and feeling the tiger start to rear up. "Go on. See what happens."

They stare at each other for a long moment, and Tally knows that Luke was telling the truth. He *can* see her – and he can also see the tiger about to pounce.

He takes a step back and then gives a quick nod to Ameet.

"Let's get out of here," he snaps. "And leave these sad losers to it."

Tally watches as they storm out of the hall and then turns to face Miles.

"Are you actually my friend, then?" he asks before she can speak, peering over the top of his glasses that have slid down his nose again. "Because I thought that you didn't like me very much."

Tally narrows her eyes. "I said that I was your friend, didn't I? I don't tell lies."

"So does that mean that you'll stand in the right place for the spotlight?" Miles persists. "That would be a very friendly thing to do because otherwise I'm going to have to reprogramme all the lights and it'll take ages."

Lucy makes a funny sound in the back of her throat like she's about to laugh, and Tally whips her head around to shoot her a warning glance before looking back at Miles.

"Yes," she tells him. "I'll stand in the right place. But not because you told me to. I'll do it because it's the right thing to do and I want to do it."

Miles nods seriously and then bends back over his lighting plan, his pencil moving lightning quick across the paper as he scrawls more notes.

"I'll catch you up outside," Tally tells Lucy and Ayesha. She waits until they've left the hall before turning back to Miles. "I'm sorry that Luke said those things to you," she tells him. "I should have stopped him sooner. He shouldn't have told you about the party – just ignore what he said about it."

Miles straightens up and gazes over Tally's shoulder, his face puzzled. "But it was true," he says. "I wasn't invited. Did you know that the world record for the largest number of people wearing those shiny cone party hats at the same time was set in 2019 in an English school? It wasn't even that many people – only one thousand, one hundred and sixty-one, which I think could be easily beaten. Not by me though – I hate the way the elastic on those hats digs into your chin skin. I like hats though. If I had to wear a hat for a party then I'd choose something else like maybe a cowboy hat or a fedora or maybe a top hat."

Tally stares at him for a moment and then starts to laugh.

"Chin skin?" she stutters. "*Chin skin?*"

Miles tilts his head to one side and lets his eyes flicker towards her. "Are you laughing at me?"

"No!" Tally tries, and fails, to control her giggles. "I'm laughing at *chin skin*. And I know exactly what you mean. It's horrible!"

"It really is." Miles hesitates and then starts laughing too. "Did they have shiny party hats at Jasmine's Zombie Laser party?"

Tally's laughter comes to an abrupt halt. Nobody has mentioned the details of the party today. Miles must have known about it all along.

"No," she tells him. "They didn't have any shiny hats. There weren't any hats at all, actually."

"Oh." Miles picks up his lighting plan and starts to walk towards the hall doors. "Not much of a party, then?"

"Not much of a party," agrees Tally.

They reach the corridor and Miles pauses. "I'm going to Koala Club," he says, not looking at Tally. "You can come if you want to."

Tally takes a deep breath and thinks about what he's suggesting. Lucy and Ayesha are waiting for her outside, and Layla is probably with them. If she goes with Miles then she isn't sure what people will think.

"You don't have to, though." The words stumble over themselves in a desperate attempt to get out of Miles's mouth. "I'm not telling you what to do. I know you don't like being told."

"I know you're not telling me," says Tally. "You're asking me, and that's different. Asking is good."

She *isn't* sure what people will think, but she *is* sure that right now, she doesn't particularly care.

WHAT MAKES A GOOD FRIEND?

A good listener – Miles isn't a big talker but I am, so we're quite a good duo.

Interesting – Miles always has some new fact to tell me.

Funny – I like a good laugh and so does Miles.

Likes doing the same things as me – it's really hard when your friend doesn't share your interests.

CHAPTER 21

The doorbell is ringing, loud and insistent.

"Tally!" Mum's voice calls up the stairs. "Your guests are starting to arrive! Come and let them in. It's pouring with rain out there."

Tally burrows further down under the duvet and pretends that she is far, far away. She doesn't care where – just anywhere that isn't this particular house on this particular day.

The bedroom door flies open and Nell stamps across the floor before yanking the covers off her head.

"What are you doing?" she demands. "Your friends are here – you can't hide in your room all afternoon."

"Yes, I can," snaps Tally, trying to pull the duvet out of Nell's hands. "I can do whatever I want to do."

Nell throws the duvet on to the floor and glares down

at Tally. "Stop being so selfish," she hisses. "Mum and Dad have planned this whole party just for you and you're being an ungrateful little brat, just for a change. Now get up and go downstairs and greet your friends."

Tally scowls at Nell, but there's no point in arguing back. If she doesn't go down now then Dad will be up here next, and there's no way that he'll let her stay in her room. Slowly, she uncurls her body and swings her legs off the bed before pulling herself up and on to the floor.

"You can't go down like that!" gasps Nell as Tally takes a step towards the door. "You look like you haven't brushed your hair for weeks!"

Tally shrugs. She hasn't – not properly, anyway. It hurts too much, so she just pulls it all back into a ponytail for school and nobody ever seems to notice.

"For goodness' sake." Nell makes a big huffing noise and rolls her eyes. "Come here."

Normally Tally would never do anything that Nell told her to do, but today, with fifty worries bouncing around her head demanding attention, she hasn't got the energy to fight. She walks across the carpet to where Nell is standing and allows her big sister to slowly, slowly pull the hairbrush through her tangles.

"That's not so bad, is it?" says Nell, her other hand

gently holding on to each lock of hair to stop the brush yanking at the roots. Tears spring into Tally's eyes, but she blinks them away quickly before Nell can see. It's not Nell's fault that every stroke of the brush feels like one thousand pins scraping into her scalp.

"No," whispers Tally. "It's not so bad."

Nell gives a few more brushes and then deftly twists Tally's hair into an elaborate plait, securing the end with an elastic band. Tally can feel each hair being tugged in an unfamiliar and painful direction, and she opens her mouth to tell Nell to take it out. But then she sees Nell smiling at her in the mirror and she shuts it again. Nell is trying to be kind. Tally understands that – even if Nell does always seem to get it wrong.

"You look great!" Nell claps her hands. "Now let's go. It's party time!"

Both girls walk towards the bedroom door and out on to the landing. Tally can hear more voices below now – it sounds like everyone is already here. Her feet slow down and she grips the top of the bannister tightly.

"It'll be fine," Nell says, pushing past her. "I always used to get a bit nervous before my birthday parties, but you'll love it once you get down there. Parties are fun! And Tally?" She turns back and gives Tally a firm look. "If nothing else then just *pretend* you're having a good time, OK? For Mum and Dad?"

Then Nell heads down the stairs, leaving Tally and her thoughts to descend on their own.

Step one. *A voice in her head is screaming that she never asked to have a party.*

Step two. Silence the voice – push it far, far away.

Step three. *Her legs want to run back to her room where it is quiet and safe.*

Step four. Plant her feet firmly on the next step and force her legs to keep moving forward.

Step five. *Her eyes are stinging with tears and her mouth is trembling with worries.*

Step six. Blink hard and put on a smile. It's not enough just not to cry – other people need her to actually look happy.

Step seven. *Parties are fun. Parties are fun.*

Step eight. Pretend, pretend, pretend.

"Happy Birthday! Open my present!"

"No – open mine first!"

"Happy Birthday, Tally! I hope you like my gift!"

Everywhere that Tally looks there are faces. And worse than the faces are the presents that are being thrust towards her from every direction. Presents wrapped in

211

paper of every colour and pattern, wrapped so tightly that she can't possibly see what's inside.

"Why don't we all go and sit down?" laughs Mum, gently steering Tally into the living room. "Girls – find a space to sit. There are some snacks on the table, and I'll go and get you some drinks."

"Is it just us coming, then?" asks Lucy, looking around the room at Layla and Ayesha. "My mum wondered why you were only having a party at home. She said that you were very brave if you were having the whole class at your house and that she'd rather splash out on a big party at the leisure centre – apparently my last party cost a *fortune*. But if it's only the four of us here then I guess a little party makes sense."

Mum smiles at Lucy, although Tally can see that the smile is one of her fake ones.

"And wouldn't life be boring if we all had the same kind of parties?" she says brightly. "Now – who would like lemonade and who would like cola? Or we have orange juice if you don't want a fizzy drink."

"Lemonade, please," says Layla.

"Me too," adds Ayesha. "Thank you."

"And what about you?" Mum asks Lucy. "What would you like?"

"Do you have any Slush Puppies?" asks Lucy. "We had Slush Puppies at my party and they were amazing!"

"We have lemonade, cola and orange juice," Mum repeats. "Although, if you don't like any of those, then I can offer you a glass of water." She looks at Lucy. "And I can probably stretch to a few ice cubes if that would help make it a little more like a Slush Puppy."

"Lemonade is fine," says Lucy, hurriedly. "Thank you, Mrs Adams."

Mum looks across at Tally. "Lemonade for you, birthday girl?"

Tally nods and Mum gives her a grin. "OK. Four lemonades coming up. We'll be back in a bit."

"Shouldn't one of us stay in here?" Dad mutters, looking at Tally as she sits stiffly in the armchair. "Just to make sure everything is OK?"

Mum shakes her head and puts her hand on his arm. "Give them a minute to settle in," she tells him. "It's far better if we leave them to it."

The door closes behind them and Tally stares at her friends. She's had them all over to her house before, of course she has – but it's always different on a birthday. There are different rules and everyone expects you to feel the way that they feel on *their* birthday, and she hates it.

"How come you only invited us?" asks Lucy, as soon as Mum and Dad are safely in the kitchen. "Everyone always invites the whole class."

Tally stares at her. That's just not true and Lucy knows it.

"I think this is great," says Layla, leaping in to defend her best friend. "It's going to be really fun!"

"Oh – I didn't mean that it wasn't fun!" says Lucy, her face screwing up with concern. "It's just a bit different, that's all."

"I didn't only invite you, anyway," says Tally, still perched on the edge of the armchair. "Mum told me to invite my friends and so I asked the three of you and Miles too." She glances towards the living room door. "He's late."

"You asked *Miles*?" Ayesha's voice is squeaky. "Why?"

"Yeah – why on earth would you invite *him* to your party?" asks Lucy. "Nobody ever invites him. I don't think he's ever been given a party invitation in his entire life!"

Tally narrows her eyes and stares at them both.

"Well now he has," she tells them. "And he's my friend."

The girls fall silent, and Tally wishes that Mum and Dad would come back in and do something to make everyone feel like they're at a *proper* party. The room feels awkward and wrong, and she doesn't know what to do about it. She has to do something, though. It's her party and she's responsible for it going right.

She can do this. She can do what Nell told her to do and pretend.

"Shall I put on a performance of *The Tally Show*?" she asks, suddenly springing to her feet and startling the other girls. "We haven't seen Tap-Dancing Terence for a while, have we? I think it's definitely time that he made an appearance!"

She clicks her heels together and leaps into the air.

"I'm siiiiiiinging in the raiiiiin," she warbles. "Just siiinging in the raiiiin!" She side steps energetically across the room and just manages to avoid crashing into Dad as he walks in with a tray of drinks.

"Careful, Tally!" Dad puts the tray down and raises an eyebrow at his daughter. "What have I told you about flinging yourself about in this room? Granny Lola's antique vase is on the mantelpiece and if it gets broken it'll be a disaster. It's irreplaceable."

Tally grinds to a halt and glares back at him, her head starting to buzz. It's bad enough that he says this kind of thing to her on a regular day, but to say it now, on her birthday and in front of her friends? That's unforgivable.

"I hate that stupid vase and I hate you," she mutters.

Her voice is very quiet, so quiet that it's barely audible. But even though the words themselves can't be heard, their tone fills the room and the words find their target. Dad's face falls, like someone has just given him a slap and over on the sofa, Tally's friends shuffle and whisper to each other.

"Who would like some crisps?" says Mum as she walks in. She takes one look at the frozen scene and launches into action. "Actually, the crisps can wait. Why doesn't everyone give Tally their gifts?"

Lucy recovers first. "Open mine!" she says, jumping up and racing across the room to give Tally a brightly wrapped present. "I got one of these for *my* birthday and it's brilliant!"

Tally sinks down on to the floor and the other girls join her.

"What is it?" she asks, staring suspiciously at the package. "Is it a game?"

"Open it and find out!" laughs Lucy. "You're going to love it."

And this is why Tally really hates birthday parties. Lucy can't possibly know whether Tally is going to love the gift or not. How *can* she know, when Tally herself has no idea? But Lucy *expects* that Tally is going to love it, which means that in about thirty seconds, she's *expecting* to see Tally react in a particular way. And that is a big problem.

Tally is not daft. She knows that when she opens a gift, the person giving the gift wants to see her looking happy or surprised or excited or amazed. And she understands why they want to see those things. After all, they've gone to all the effort of giving her something – so the least she can do is be grateful. And she *is* grateful. She really, truly is. It's just that, sometimes, she thinks that the whole present-giving thing is less to do with the person receiving the gift and more to do with the gift-giver. It's as if they think that along with the present, they've purchased the right to see her do things in a certain way.

Say the right things.

Make the right faces.

And Tally can do these things, but she needs a heads-up: a bit of advance warning about what emotion it is that she's supposed to be showing. Because otherwise it can all go a little bit wrong, like the time she got ready to be completely amazed and awe-struck by Auntie Tish's Christmas present, and it turned out to be a very boring pair of socks stuffed inside an equally boring mug. Her beaming face and excited squealing about how awesome the mug was and how she'd wanted a pair of socks *for ever* turned out to be completely the wrong reaction, and Dad ended up telling her to stop being sarcastic and that a simple *thank you* would have been fine.

As far as Tally is concerned, if her birthday was really about *her* then she'd be allowed to open all her presents in the privacy of her own room where she could just enjoy them without worrying about what her face was supposed to be doing. But it isn't about her, and so she's started to develop some strategies to make the whole, torturous process a little easier.

"Is it something to wear?" she asks, poking the gift with a finger. "No – it's too hard."

"Just open it!" says Layla. "Then you can have mine next."

"Is it a craft-making kit?" she persists, giving the parcel a shake. "Oh – I can hear something rattling. It sounds like the bracelet making kit I got last year! It wasn't very good because the bracelets all broke after a week."

She carefully pulls off the paper, trying hard not to rip it more than is absolutely necessary, and pulls out a box, her face triumphant. "I was right! It's the exact same kit! Thank you, Lucy!"

Lucy's face is a bit red and she mumbles something under her breath, which Tally can't hear. Ayesha gives her a sympathetic look, but then Layla hands Tally her gift and she hasn't got time to wonder about what's wrong with Lucy because the entire process has to start all over again.

Birthdays are exhausting and unpredictable, and Tally is exceedingly glad that they only come around once a year.

Once the present opening has been endured, Mum takes them all into the kitchen. She's set up the table with a whole load of ingredients and a small chalkboard sign, which reads *Pizza Parlour*. Dad is standing by the island holding a pile of aprons, wearing a tall, white chef's hat on his head.

"Welcome to Tally's Pizza Parlour," he says, drawling his words in a way that Tally suspects is supposed to sound Italian. "If you would kindly put on an apron and stand behind a mixing bowl, then we will begin by making the pizza dough."

The girls dash across to grab an apron, and before long, all four of them are following Dad's instructions on how to make the perfect dough.

"I've never made pizza before," says Lucy, pummeling the dough in her hands. "We just get it out of the freezer and put it in the oven. This is brilliant!"

"Are we going to add toppings?" asks Ayesha, rolling her dough into a large, flat circle.

"Of course," Mum tells her. "Look – there's lots to choose from."

She points at the kitchen table, where Tally can see bowls filled with cheese, tomatoes, olives, pepperoni, ham and pineapple as well as strips of peppers, mushrooms and tiny pieces of bacon.

"That's amazing!" says Layla, her eyes widening. "Can we choose whatever we want?"

"Whatever you want," Dad assures her. "More is definitely more when it comes to creating the perfect pizza."

Pizza bases made, the girls move on to adding their toppings, their chatter filling the room. Tally joins in, but she keeps looking at the clock on the wall and then towards the door, and eventually Layla notices.

"I don't think he's coming," she whispers, as Lucy and Ayesha engage in a spirited debate about whether mushrooms have any place on a pizza. "I'm sorry, Tally."

Tally shrugs. "I don't care," she whispers back. "It's better just with us, anyway."

And then she crosses her fingers behind her back and says a silent apology in her head, because telling a lie on your birthday can't ever be good.

Once the pizzas are in the oven, Mum tells them all

to head back into the living room.

"You can start watching the film now," she tells them. "And if you promise to be super careful then you can have a carpet picnic and eat your pizzas on the floor while you keep watching."

"This party is the best," Lucy tells her as they all pile out of the room. "Thanks!"

"Did you hear that?" Mum grins at Tally. "Your party is the best, apparently."

Tally looks across at where Dad is starting to clear up the mess.

"I'm sorry," she tells him quietly. "I didn't mean to—"

"—It's OK," he says lightly. "I know that you didn't. Now go and have fun and we'll bring the pizzas through once they're cooked."

Go and have fun.

This party is the best.

Tally wishes that she felt that way, but it's just so difficult. Even when Dad is being so kind and Mum is trying so hard to make it all work, her brain just won't stop whirring with questions and thoughts and worries.

The doorbell rings just as Tally is about to follow the others into the living room. She hesitates and then pulls the front door open.

"This is for you." Two hands thrust a bag in her face, and she steps backwards in surprise. "It's a book, in case you were wondering. The pages are a bit creased and there's a rip on the front cover because I've already read it a ton of times, but that's how I know that it's good and that you'll like it. I wouldn't give you a book that I haven't read, just in case it's a bit rubbish."

He pauses for a second to catch his breath.

"Are you coming to my party?" Tally asks, stepping forward. "You've missed making the pizza, but you can share some of mine if you like."

Miles shuffles his feet and stares at the ground.

"I hate parties." He pushes the bag into her hands and turns away. "Take care of it," he says. "It's my favourite book in the world, and I've had it for a really long time."

"So why are you giving it to *me*, then?" Tally shakes her head in confusion. "If it's your favourite? You shouldn't give something away that's important to you."

Miles stops and Tally isn't sure that he's going to speak.

"I hate parties," he says eventually, his voice muffled by the pounding rain. "I liked being invited though."

Tally watches as he plods away, his hood pulled up

against the torrential rain.

"Why did you come over now?" she shouts, as he reaches the gate. "You could have given it to me at school tomorrow."

Miles swivels round, a frown on his face.

"It's your birthday *today*," he yells back. "I had to come today. Tomas helped me. He's my big brother and sometimes he's a pain, but today he's being quite nice. We have to go now because he's off to see his girlfriend and he has smelly feet so he needs to have a shower first."

"Tell everyone, why don't you?" Tomas ruffles his hand through Miles's hair and grins at Tally. "Happy birthday, Tally."

"Happy birthday to you too!" calls Tally, which for some reason makes him laugh. And then they're gone and she closes the front door, sliding down on to the carpet to peek inside the bag that Miles has given her.

Not that she needs to look. She already knows what's inside, and the fact that he has given it to her makes her feel warm and safe and maybe a little bit sad but also, yes – happy.

"What's that?" asks Nell, coming down the stairs. "Who gave you an ancient old book for your birthday?"

Tally stands up, hugging the precious gift tightly.

"My friend," she says, and then she walks into the living room, where the other girls are already engrossed in the movie. Tally sinks down next to them but instead of watching the screen, she flicks through the pages of Miles's very first copy of the *Guinness Book Of World Records*, finally ready to sit down and enjoy the rest of her day.

Her way.

CHAPTER 22

It seems like for ever since Tally was last at the stables, but as soon as she steps inside it feels utterly familiar. Layla hasn't come with her this time, but she doesn't mind. She likes spending time with her best friend, but today she doesn't want any distraction. It will just be her and Peaches and nothing else.

"You came back then?" Ginny steps out of one of the stalls, an empty bucket in her hands. "I was wondering where you'd got to. I thought you'd gone off us – like those flighty young things that turn up once and can't cope with the smells and the muck."

Tally swallows and shakes her head furiously.

"I'd be here every day if I could," she says, her words rushing out in a hurry. "But Mum says it's too expensive for me to come all the time."

Ginny makes a huffing sound and thrusts the bucket at Tally.

"Well, you're here now so we might as well make the most of you. Peaches needs feeding – go on down to the end of the barn and fill this with food."

She marches off and after a moment's hesitation, Tally does as she is instructed, filling the bucket and then staggering back under the heavy weight to the stall where Peaches is waiting.

On the other side of the gate, Ginny is whispering quietly into the horse's ear. Tally waits patiently, watching the way that Peaches seems to quieten and still as Ginny runs her hands over the horse's flank. Eventually, the stable owner notices her and beckons her in.

"Horses need to be spoken to calmly," she says, taking the bucket from Tally. "Just because they're wonderful, strong animals doesn't mean that they like to be shouted at. I won't abide any raised voices in my stables – that's rule number one."

"I wish it was rule number one at my school," mutters Tally, sidling along the wall until she's next to Peaches' nose.

"Rule number two is that we never force a horse to do something it is afraid of doing," continues Ginny, emptying the bucket into a trough. "Horses are creatures of habit – they like having the same routines and knowing what to expect. No good can ever come from frightening them with unpredictable behaviour."

"I have to do scary things all the time." Tally reaches out her hand and then pauses, glancing at Ginny who gives a short nod. "And not knowing what's happening next is the worst feeling in the whole world."

She strokes along the side of Peaches' nose, and the horse nuzzles against her hand. The stall is quiet as Ginny finishes her jobs, leaving Tally in peace for a while and then, once she's done, she opens the gate and gestures for Tally to walk through.

"Let's have a chat," she says and it isn't a request. With a reluctant look back at where Peaches is standing, Tally follows Ginny outside, blinking as her eyes adjust to the bright sunshine.

The stable owner is standing near a lush, green paddock where several ponies are being put through their paces. Tally walks up and stands beside her, mimicking the way she leans against the fence on her elbows. And then she waits.

And waits.

And waits a bit more, because despite the request

for a chat, it would seem that Ginny isn't much of a fan of talking. The silence is nice though – nothing like the awkward, scary silence when Miss Balogun asks the class a question and nobody puts their hand up.

"I wish that I was a horse." Tally breathes out, a long contented sigh as she listens to the sound of the ponies whinnying. "I'd never have to pretend to be someone I'm not."

Ginny turns slightly in her direction, although Tally notices that she doesn't look directly at her eyes.

"What do you mean?" she asks. "Who are you pretending to be?"

Tally shrugs. "A normal person. A good person. Someone that other people will like. Someone like *them*."

Ginny frowns and turns back to gaze at the ponies. "And who are you really?"

Tally hesitates. This isn't the kind of conversation that she is used to having. She works really hard to hide the person she is inside, especially with strangers. But there is something about this Ginny woman that makes her want to tell the truth. Maybe it's because she *is* a stranger – or maybe it's because she knows, somehow, that Ginny will get it.

"I'm just a bit different," she says quietly. "I've always

been different, but now I've found out that there's an actual reason for it and I don't really know what to do about it."

Ginny makes a sniffing noise. "Maybe you could stop worrying about trying to be like everyone else," she says, "and just be like you."

A prickle of disappointment flits across Tally's face. She was wrong. Ginny doesn't get it any more than the rest of them do.

"It's not that easy," she mutters. "You wouldn't understand. Nobody understands."

Ginny glances down at her. "You're not the only autistic girl in the world," she says, her voice light. "I understand a whole lot more than you might think."

Tally's stomach flips over and she clutches hard on to the fence. It's hard to know which is the more shocking – the fact that Ginny knows about her, or the casual way she says that *word*.

"Did my mum tell you?" she whispers, the betrayal making her eyes sting. "She promised that she wouldn't tell anyone else."

Ginny shakes her head and focuses her attention once more on the ponies. "Did you know that wild horses organize themselves into herds and that they can recognize each other? They use body signals and cues to identify the horses in their group."

Tally blinks hard, trying not to let the tears fall. Coming to the stables was her one good thing, and now Mum has ruined even that.

"I've always preferred horses to people," continues Ginny. "And just like horses, I can recognize the people in my herd." She bends over and plucks a long blade of grass that she proceeds to rub between her fingers. "I know that you are autistic because I'm autistic too – and you very much remind me of myself at your age. That's why I put you with Peaches – I knew that you had passion and fire and strength. Your mother never said a word."

Tally gawps at Ginny, her mouth open.

"You have autism?" she says. "You? But you have all this!"

She waves her hand around, taking in the stables and the paddocks and the horses.

Ginny makes a snorting noise. "I'm very lucky," she agrees. "Although I had to work extra hard to get through school and then gain my Stable Management and Equine Care qualifications at college. It wasn't always easy, but I knew what I wanted to do and I worked every weekend at my local stables to get experience. And even though I find dealing with people quite tricky, being around the horses all day more than makes up for it."

"But you don't look autistic," says Tally, knowing even as the words leave her mouth that they make absolutely no sense.

"Neither do you," shoots back Ginny. "Anyway, what is an autistic person supposed to look like?"

Tally shrugs. She doesn't have an answer for that.

"You said that you want to be like everyone else," says Ginny. "And I understand that. I have days when it just seems easier to put on a mask and pretend."

"You have a mask?" Tally asks, surprised. "So do I! Mine is a tiger mask and when I wear it I feel like nobody can hurt me. What's yours like?"

Ginny's mouth flickers. "I haven't got a tiger mask," she confesses. "Although that does sound pretty great. This is my mask, right here." She waves a hand at her own face. "Sometimes I take a deep breath and I hide how I'm really feeling behind a huge smile. And even if it's too noisy or people are having a conversation that confuses me or I just feel quiet inside and as if I need some time alone, I act like everything is fine."

Tally nods so quickly that the world blurs for a moment. "I do that too!"

"Everyone does it now and again," Ginny tells her. "But

the most important thing to remember is that you can't stay hidden behind a mask for long. If you don't let the real Tally out, then eventually you're going to be so tired and burnt out from all the masking that things are going to go wrong."

Tally stares at her. "What do you mean?"

Ginny exhales slowly. "You have to be brave, Tally. You have to love the person you are and embrace the fact that you're a bit different."

"Sometimes I feel a *lot* different," Tally points out. "And sometimes I feel like I mess everything up and make life hard for everyone who knows me. I can be quite hard to love, I think." She pauses for a moment. "Do you love the person who *you* are, then?"

Ginny goes quiet and Tally can't tell if she's gazing at the ponies or far off into the sky. In the paddock, two of the ponies start nuzzling each other and Tally watches, mesmerized, as one of them rests its head over the neck of the other. Whinnies and nickers float across the grass, and the warm air has a tang of fresh hay. Despite the unexpected conversation, Tally feels more peaceful than she has in a while.

"I don't always love the person I am when I'm hiding behind my mask." Ginny's voice is quiet.

Tally clambers up on to the second rung of the fence. "Don't hide then," she suggests, lifting her arms up like she's flying. "Just be you. I think *you* are brilliant, just the way you are."

Ginny glances down at the ground, and when she looks back up, her eyes are glistening. "Thank you, Tally," she says quietly. "That means an awful lot."

"Ginny!" The shout comes from the stables and when Tally turns, she sees Saira beckoning from the open door. "The delivery is here. Do you want to check it over before I sign for it?"

"Give me one minute," calls back Ginny, and then she climbs up on to the fence, next to Tally. "You've given me some excellent advice," she says. "Can I give you some in return?"

Tally nods but doesn't take her eyes off the ponies.

"It took me a long time to learn that the true me is somebody worth knowing," says Ginny. "Somebody worth loving. Don't wait as long as I have to appreciate what makes you special."

And then she jumps down and marches off to the stables, leaving Tally alone in the sunshine, with one million thoughts whizzing round her head.

All of which are pretty good.

CHAPTER 23

Tally can hear the buzz in the classroom from halfway up the stairs. Excited voices float down the stairs and she picks up her pace, keen to find out what is going on. Pushing through the doorway, she scans the room and sees that the majority of the class is huddled in a group around one of the desks.

"Hey, Layla!" she calls, spotting her friend in the midst of the crowd.

At the sound of her voice, the chattering stops, and everyone turns to look her way. The air fizzes with a strange tension, the way it sometimes does before a fight in the playground, and Tally's feet hesitate, reluctant to go any further.

"Tally!" calls Jasmine, beckoning her towards the group. "Come and see! You're never going to believe it!"

"Uh-oh," mutters one of the boys. "This is going to be interesting…"

Tally swallows hard and then slowly walks forward. People step to the side as she passes, peering through the fog of confusion to see the source of all the commotion.

And then she's at the desk and everything snaps into a clear reality.

"Hi!" Carrie's beaming face looks up at Tally. "I'm back!"

Tally stares at her in disbelief. "But you're ill," she tells her. "You're not coming into school until at least next week."

Carrie laughs. "I got better!" she says, standing up and spreading her arms wide. "Isn't it great?"

"You're back just in time to play Little Red in the production!" squeals Jasmine, clapping her hands. "It's perfect!"

"No." Tally is aware that everyone is looking at her, but she can't let this happen. "*I'm* Little Red."

"Here we go," says Luke, elbowing Ameet. "I told you that she'd kick off."

"Nobody is kicking off," snaps Layla. "And shut up, Luke. It's none of your business."

"OK, everybody, let's all sit down." Miss Balogun sweeps into the classroom before anyone can say anything else. "We've got a lot to sort out today, so let's get going."

She sits down at her desk and pulls out the register.

"Good morning, Lucy," she calls. "Good morning, Ameet."

Tally sink downs into her seat and stares at the table.

"Good morning, Jasmine," continues the teacher. "And good morning, Carrie! We're all glad to have you back, aren't we, year six?"

Twenty-nine voices murmur their agreement. One voice remains silent.

Once the register is finished, Miss Balogun looks out at the class. "So, we've got one last day of rehearsing and then the production is tomorrow afternoon. There's still some painting to do on the backdrop, and we need to make sure that everyone has the correct costume and props."

"Miss!" Jasmine's hand shoots into the air. "Is Carrie going to have her part back?"

"It's not *her* part," mutters Tally quietly. She plunges her hand into her pocket and pulls out the ladybird necklace, keeping it hidden below the desk while tipping it from one hand to the other.

"That's a very good question," Miss Balogun tells Jasmine, casting her gaze from Carrie to Tally and then back to Carrie. "And one that I think we need to address immediately. Right – I'm going to talk to Carrie and Tally, and the rest of you need to get out our class book and start reading up to page…"

Tally zones out, focusing on the necklace in her hand. If ever she needed some good luck, she needs some now, and she closes her eyes, letting the lucky charm glide between her fingers.

Please let me keep the part of Little Red.

Please let Miss Balogun choose me.

And then the necklace falls. Tally feels it slide through her fingers and she scrabbles to catch it, but it slinks and slips out of her grasp, landing on the floor with a light, metallic tinkle, so quiet that it can barely be heard.

The gasp that comes from Layla's mouth is harder to ignore. Tally opens her eyes and sees Layla staring, her eyes darting from Tally to the necklace by her feet. Quick as a flash, Tally reaches down and picks it up, encasing the ladybird inside her fist and bracing herself for the cries of outrage.

The pointing fingers.

The shouts accusing her of being the thief.

Nothing happens.

The teacher is still talking and the room is suddenly unbearably hot, but nobody reacts. Tally risks a glance at

Layla, whose face is one big question mark, but her friend doesn't say a word. When Tally sneaks a look around, the other kids are either busy opening their reading books or doodling on a scrap piece of paper or, in Miles's case, staring out of the window with an expression that says he would far rather be out there than stuck inside this classroom.

Nobody except Layla has seen.

She's got away with it.

"Girls!" Miss Balogun is beckoning to Tally and Carrie. "Let's have a quick chat out in the corridor." She walks to the door and turns to look at the rest of the class. "I will be listening, so no messing about," she warns.

"You took it?" Layla whispers, leaning closer to Tally. "How could you?"

"Come on, Tally!" calls Miss Balogun. "This will only take a few minutes."

Tally pushes back her seat and stands up. She doesn't know what Miss Balogun is going to say, but she does know that she can't lose her part. Not now. She reaches the door and turns to look back at Layla. Her best friend, the person who is always there for her, no matter what, gives her a sad look and shakes her head before turning away.

Maybe she hasn't got away with it after all.

★

"You can't give her the part back," Tally blurts out, the moment that she's outside the classroom. "It's mine now and she isn't even supposed to be here."

Miss Balogun holds her hand up. "Hang on a second," she tells her. "I want us to talk about this properly, and that means that we have to listen to each other." She turns to face Carrie. "What do you think, Carrie? Do you even *want* to play Little Red after so much time off school? You've missed a lot of rehearsals."

Carrie's face goes a bit pink. "I've been working really hard on learning the lines," she says earnestly. "And I can still remember where I have to stand on the stage and everything."

"OK." Miss Balogun nods. "Well, this is slightly tricky. Tally has also been working really hard to learn the part, and I'm not sure that it would be fair for me to take that away from her."

"It definitely wouldn't be fair," agrees Tally.

"I understand," says Carrie at the same time.

Miss Balogun's lips press tightly together, and her forehead scrunches up.

"I think, on reflection, that we're going to have to let Tally make the decision," she says slowly. "Carrie – you head back into class and give us a moment, please."

She waits until the other girl has gone and then looks at Tally.

"I know that this is hard," she says simply. "And I also know how important it was to you to play the part of Little Red. But I also know that Carrie was excited about it too."

Tally shrugs. It isn't hard at all. Miss Balogun has said that it's up to her to choose, and it's an easy choice to make.

"I want to be Little Red," she tells her. "Carrie can help Miles with the lights."

A flicker passes across the teacher's face, but it's so fast that Tally can't work out what it means. Then she nods and gestures towards the classroom door.

"Very well," she says. "I'll tell Carrie that you are to have the main part – she's going to be disappointed, but I'm sure she'll understand."

And then she disappears back into the classroom, leaving Tally in the corridor wondering why she isn't feeling as happy as she really should be.

CHAPTER 24

A school day is six and a half hours, but this day feels like it has been going on for ever. Tally has tried to talk to Layla, but her friend won't even look in her direction, never mind actually speak to her. *Nobody* really wants to speak to her – they haven't got time in between frantically painting the set and organizing the costumes and trying to make Carrie feel better. Tally keeps seeing them staring at her and then whispering to each other, and even though nobody says it to her face, she knows exactly what is going on.

Nobody thinks she's good enough to play Little Red, not now that Carrie is back.

At the end of the day, Mum is waiting for her outside in the playground.

"I've been into the school office," she says excitedly.

"And collected our tickets for tomorrow afternoon. We're in the front row, which means that we won't miss a single moment of your debut performance!"

"Be quiet!" snarls Tally. "My head hurts and your stupid talking is making it worse."

Mum frowns. "That's very rude," she tells Tally. "And there was no need for it. Say sorry, please."

Tally marches out through the school gates and then waits for Mum to catch her up. She might not want to listen to Mum's ridiculous chatter, but she also doesn't want to risk getting kidnapped by a stranger, which is one of her biggest worries.

"Tally." Mum clearly isn't giving up. "You need to apologize."

"I'm *so, so* sorry." Tally's voice is a growl, low and menacing. "But you can't blame me. I'm autistic – I can't help it."

"We'll talk about this at home," snaps Mum. "But that black cloud above your head has got to go!" Then she strides along the pavement, her shoulders rigid with anger. Tally stalks behind her, wondering how she's supposed to get rid of a cloud that she never asked to appear in the first place. And with every step she takes, the effort of keeping it all together builds more and more, until she can feel the pressure from her toes to the tips of her hair.

The moment that the front door closes behind them and she's finally safe, the volcano erupts.

"I'm never going back to school!" She flings her bag into the corner and glares at Mum. "And you can't make me!"

Mum opens her mouth and starts to speak, but Tally can't hear her. She can't hear anything except the loud, insistent noises in her head, and even they are too overwhelming to make any sense. All she knows is that she's finally reached breaking point and she has to escape from the turmoil inside; the confusion and chaos that's created by having to spend all day, every day being somebody else.

Acting like she gets the joke when everyone else is laughing.

Her shoes fly through the air and thud against the opposite wall.

Pretending that the hurtful comments bounce off her when really, they pierce her skin.

Her hands pummel the door, hard, harder, hardest – but she doesn't feel a thing.

Trying to zone out the constant loudness of school without drawing attention to herself.

Her feet pound against the wooden floorboards,

taking her from one room to the next as they try to outrun the pain.

Doing whatever she can to be like the rest of them.

But what was the point? Layla saw the necklace and now she knows. She knows that Tally isn't who she's been desperately trying to be. The truth is out there and it's difficult and messy and real – just like Tally is.

She reaches the bathroom, and by the time Mum gets there, Tally is a tiny, curled-up comma on the floor. A comma in a long list of problems that she doesn't know how to solve.

It is some time later when she's eventually ready to sit up, and even longer before she can move from under the sink. Mum lets her take her time. The lava subsides and the volcano calms and Tally's heart returns to something that feels a bit more regular.

"Would you like to wash your face?" asks Mum, her voice low and quiet.

Tally nods and Mum helps her to stand up. Her face is hot and tear-stained, although she doesn't remember crying. Mum dampens a flannel and holds it out towards Tally, but Tally can't move. It's like her body has forgotten what it's supposed to be doing.

"Shall I help you?"

Another nod and Mum gently wipes Tally's tears away before reaching out to take her hand.

"Let's get you on to the sofa," she suggests and then slowly leads Tally down the stairs and towards the living room. As they walk through the house, Tally can see the aftermath of the chaos, but Mum doesn't say a thing.

"The wall…" whispers Tally, as they pass through the hall and she sees the damage that her muddy shoes have caused.

"We'll clean it up later," says Mum. "Together, OK? For now you can have a bit of a rest – I bet you're tired, aren't you?"

Mum is right. She *is* tired – the kind of tired she imagines a person would be after climbing a mountain. Tally sinks against the cushions and closes her eyes, transporting herself to the stables where everything is good. And thinking about the stables reminds her of Ginny and the advice that she gave her.

That things are going to go wrong if she keeps on hiding who she really is.

It isn't until several hours later that Mum calls her into the kitchen. Tally takes a deep breath and then pushes open the door. She knew that the telling-off would be coming and in a way it's almost a relief – she's spent the last two hours watching *Peppa Pig* episodes, but she hasn't really been able to relax, not with knowing that they've still got to have *the conversation*.

She lowers herself on to a chair and starts to tap her foot on the floor in a complicated rhythm that matches her pulse.

"Before you say anything, I can't help having bad behaviour," she starts, figuring that she might as well get her say in first. "It's not my fault."

Mum stares at her for a moment and then sits down opposite.

"Nobody is saying that you're *bad*, Tally," she tells her. "And what happened earlier wasn't really about your *behaviour*, was it? I don't think you were choosing to feel and act that way."

Tally shudders. No way would anyone ever choose to feel as out of control as she sometimes does.

"Having an autistic meltdown isn't the same thing as having a temper tantrum," Mum continues. "And I know that things are really tough for you right now, but we need to talk about a few things. And the first of those things is the fact that you only use the word *autism* when you're telling us that something isn't your fault."

"Are you saying that autism *is* my fault?" hurls

back Tally.

Mum sighs. "No, I'm not. Partly because having autism is an aspect of you that you can't control, but mostly because autism is not a *fault*." She stares at her daughter. "Autism is not the problem, Tally. It's a reason for the way you feel – and not something to feel ashamed of."

Tally stares at her, remembering something else from the stables.

The way that Ginny used the word *autism* like it wasn't something wrong.

"I know that you've only been able to see the negative things," continues Mum. "But autism comes with a whole load of great stuff too, you know? Lots of autistic people have gone on to do wonderful things in life, and sometimes, their successes come from the things that they're passionate about."

"Like who?" sniffs Tally, not really believing her. There's Ginny, of course – but Mum doesn't even know that she's autistic so she can't mean her.

Mum tilts her head to one side and starts ticking off names on her fingers.

"People think that Albert Einstein and Mozart were autistic," she says. "And maybe also Leonardo Da Vinci and Charles Darwin. And did you know that the man who created Pokémon is autistic? He used to love collecting insects when he was a little boy, and he wanted to give other kids the chance to experience the same excitement."

Tally tucks this piece of information away in her head, ready to share with Miles tomorrow. Then she thinks about what Mum has just said.

"But they're all men," she says slowly. "What about the girls?"

Mum smiles and leans forward. "I've been wondering about that myself," she tells her. "So I did a bit of research, and guess what? Amazing autistic girls are out there too. There's Greta Thunberg and an English actress called Lizzy Clark, who was in a film called *Dustbin Baby*. That film was special because it was one of the first times an autistic person was chosen to play the part of an autistic character – and that isn't something that happens very often. It's often a non-autistic actor who is paid to act in an autistic way."

"That's not right." Tally frowns. "How is someone without autism supposed to know what an autistic person feels like? They can't pretend to be them when they don't even know."

Mum smiles gently. "You're right. They really can't."

The room is quiet for a few moments, and Tally's

attention is caught by the dust motes dancing in the rays of the sun as they stream through the window.

"One of the most famous autistic people in the world is a woman." Mum stands up and walks across the kitchen to pick up the kettle. "Her name is Temple Grandin and she's an animal behaviourist. She wasn't diagnosed with autism until she was an adult, but the things she has shared about her own experiences of autism have made her a bit of a hero."

Tally leans forward, intrigued. "Like what?"

Mum turns on the tap. "Well, she invented the hug box, for one thing."

"The what?"

"The hug box." Mum turns to grin at Tally. "Only she called it her *squeeze machine*. Temple Grandin watched cattle being held in a squeeze chute and noticed that being held calmed them down. She wondered if being tightly squeezed might help with some of *her* sensory issues and anxieties, because she knew that tight pressure made her feel calm. So she invented the hug box, for people to get a hug whenever they want, because sometimes, having a hug from another person can be a bit overwhelming."

Tally nods. On some days she loves being hugged by Mum, but on other days it just feels uncomfortable and too much.

"That's still only three, though," she says, drumming her fingers on the table. "It's not very many. Are there any other autistic girls?"

Mum nods. "Of course there are. It's just that girls often take a lot longer to get an autism diagnosis. People don't always understand that autism in girls can look quite different to autism in boys, which is a bit daft really when most people know that one autistic person is not like any other autistic person."

Tally thinks about that. It definitely makes sense, and maybe it explains why she and Miles are both so different, even though they're both autistic.

"So," Tally looks at Mum. "What you're saying is that I'm going to be either famous or a genius, then?"

Mum makes a sound that is a combination of a snort and a laugh.

"Not necessarily," she tells Tally. "What I'm saying is that you are *you*." She pauses and smiles. "You are one of a kind, my wonderful girl. There is nobody else on the planet exactly like you. And being autistic is a part of that."

Tally stares down at the table. It's all very well her own mother thinking that she's wonderful, but what's the point when nobody else thinks that? What's the point when even now, when everything has worked out brilliantly and tomorrow afternoon she's going to be stepping out on to the stage in the lead role, she isn't happy?

"I'm sorry that I was rude to you earlier," she says quietly. "It's just that everything is going wrong and I don't know what to do."

And then she opens her mouth and tells Mum the whole story – about being given the job of sorting the lights with Miles and how she wasn't even given the role of Little Red until Carrie went off sick, but now Carrie is back and she wants the part back and it's up to Tally to choose.

"And now nobody thinks I'm good enough to even be Little Red, which is really unfair because I am." She blinks hard to stop the tears that are threatening to spill down her face. "At least, I thought I was. But maybe that's not right either. Or maybe it's just that I don't deserve it because I mess everything up?"

Mum walks over and places her hand on top of Tally's.

"It sounds like there's a lot going on in your head," she says gently. "And Miss Balogun is right – this has to be your choice. I can't tell you what to do. But, Tally? I *can* tell you that you are absolutely good enough, in every way. You work hard and you do your very best to be kind, and when it goes wrong you always try to make it better."

A tear escapes and slides down Tally's cheek.

"Why is it always so hard?" she sniffs. "Why is it me that has to be different? Why can't things just work out for me? Why do I have to be the weird one who always gets it wrong?"

Mum opens her arms and Tally steps forward, letting Mum hold her tightly.

"You are lots of things," she murmurs into Tally's ear. "But *weird or wrong* are not one of them. Tell me another word that describes who you are."

Tally snuffles and doesn't speak, but Mum isn't giving up. "OK – if it's too tricky to think of a word that describes you then tell me something that you've done recently that makes you feel proud of who you are."

She lets go of Tally and takes a step back to gaze at her daughter's face. "Come on, Tally. What about the way you stepped in for Carrie and learnt all the lines for Little Red?"

Mum just doesn't get it. Tally was proud about that, but not any more. Not now that she's really thought about it. Mum wouldn't think this was something to proud of either, if she knew about the lucky charm necklace that Tally found on the floor.

She sniffs and opens her mouth to tell Mum that there isn't anything she's done that makes her proud. And then she remembers Miles.

"I stood up for my friend," she whispers. "I stopped a bully from being unkind."

Mum's eyes sparkle, like a firework on bonfire night.

"Was it easy to do that?" she asks.

Tally shakes her head quickly. "No. It was really hard and my legs felt shaky, and I was worried about what everyone would think."

"So why did you step in?"

Tally breathes out loudly, remembering that day. "It was the right thing to do," she says. "That's all."

Mum nods. "It's like I said. There are lots of words to describe you."

The front door crashes open as Nell races in. Mum raises an eyebrow at Tally. "I think it might be time for a snack," she says. "Supper is going to be quite late tonight!"

Tally walks over to the back door. "I'm going outside," she tells Mum. "I need to think about some stuff."

Mum smiles at her. "What can I do to help?" she asks.

"Nothing." Tally pulls the door open and glances back over her shoulder. "I think I have to figure this out on my own this time."

Mum nods thoughtfully. "I think you do, too."

And then Nell barrels into the kitchen, and Tally takes the opportunity to slip outside into the garden. There's only one place she can go when she needs to think properly, and even though she hasn't been there for weeks, she knows that it will be waiting for her, private and quiet and safe.

CHAPTER 25

It's still warm outside in the garden, but Tally doesn't want to sit in the sunshine. She walks down the path, past the apple tree, and then she turns left and bends down so that she can scuttle under the low, sweeping branches of the willow tree and into her den.

Dad helped her to make it several summers ago. They spent days propping old branches against the trunk and creating a secret hideaway where she could come whenever she wanted to be on her own. At this time of year, when the leaves of the willow tree block out the rest of the garden, it's even more peaceful and hidden. Tally drops to her knees and crawls through the gap.

Now she can think.

"Tally!"

Nell's voice breaks through the silence before she's

even able to think one tiny thought. "Are you in there?"

Tally clamps her lips closed and holds her breath. Maybe if she doesn't reply then her annoying big sister will leave her alone.

The sound of footsteps comes closer and then the branches are parted, letting sunlight through onto the dank, dark ground where Tally is sitting.

Nell's face appears in the gap. "There you are! Didn't you hear me calling you?"

Tally scowls. "Leave me alone."

Nell scowls back. "Charming. I guess you don't want the treat that I've brought you, then?"

She starts to shuffle back on her knees, but Tally reaches out a hand to stop her.

"What treat?" she asks. "And why?"

Nell's mouth turns up at the corners and she pauses, reaching into her pocket and pulling out a badly wrapped chocolate bar.

"You've already had some!" complains Tally, staring suspiciously at the half-eaten snack.

Nell raises an eyebrow. "Do you want it or not? Cos if you do then you'd better let me in – I'm not crouching out here all day."

Tally inches backwards, creating just enough space for

Nell to enter the den. Her sister thrusts the chocolate bar into her hands and then looks around.

"It's a bit cramped in here, isn't it?"

Tally nods, chocolate already smeared around her lips. "It used to be bigger," she mumbles through a mouthful. "I think it got smaller."

"So what's going on then?" asks Nell, pulling her knees up close to her chest. "Mum said that you're having a tough time."

Tally stops eating and looks down at the ground. There's a tiny ant making its way across the dirt, struggling to carry a piece of leaf that's three times the size of its body. It doesn't give up though, and as she watches it's joined by another ant, and then another, all marching with a purpose as if they know exactly what is expected of them.

"All I wanted was to get the main role in the production," she says. "And now I've got what I wanted but everything is still difficult and wrong. So what am I supposed to do?"

Nell shrugs. "You might have got what you wanted, but maybe that wasn't what you needed," she tells her. "Wanting and needing are not the same thing."

Tally narrows her eyes and pushes her foot into the

dirt, being careful not to squish the ants. "That's stupid," she snaps. "And it doesn't even make any sense."

Nell's face scrunches up, which Tally knows means that she's thinking really hard. "It's a bit like when you say that you *can't* do something but other people think what you're really saying is that you *won't*. It might sound like a small thing, but it makes all the difference. You said that everything is wrong, yeah?"

Tally nods.

"You got what you *want*, but it hasn't made everything OK. So what do you *need*?"

"To make things right." Tally's voice is a whisper, but Nell hears her anyway and nods.

"OK. So do that."

Tally whips her head up and glares at her sister. "Do you think it's easy? Because it isn't, OK? It's not easy making things better and it's not easy being me. It's OK for you – you're not autistic."

Nell glares back at her. "It's not easy being me either," she states. "It's not easy being *anyone*, Tally. And I know that you're autistic, but that's not the only word to describe who you are. And you need to figure out who you are if you're going to figure out how you can solve your problems."

"Did Mum send you out here to have this conversation?" snarls Tally. "Because I'm getting a little bit sick of people telling me that I'm all these words but never telling me what any of them are."

"I could tell you a few of them," shouts Nell, getting to her knees. "Like stubborn and irritating."

"Well, you're annoying and bossy and a total pain!" yells back Tally.

The two sisters glower at each other for a few seconds and then Nell's face softens.

"You're also creative and fun," she says. "And tenacious. You always keep going until you achieve whatever it is you set out to do."

Tally huffs. "I suppose you're not too bad," she acknowledges, and Nell snorts with laughter.

"I guess that's as good as I'm going to get," she says, grinning at Tally and shuffling backwards out of the den. "I'll try not to let it go to my head."

And then she's gone, and Tally is left alone in peace to finally do some thinking.

But all she can think about is what Nell just said to her.

You need to figure out who you are.

So, who is she?

★

The sun has started to dip in the sky, but Tally hasn't moved an inch. She's sitting inside the den, drawing shapes in the soil with her finger and trying to let her head calm down. The problem is that her brain just won't settle long enough for her to make sense of anything. Thoughts and words and images are hurtling around her head, and the more she tries to make them stay still, the faster they go.

Stubborn.

Irritating.

Tally's finger scrawls the words into the dirt.

Creative.

Fun.

Tenacious.

Her finger writes faster as she remembers Nell's words.

Wonderful.

Kind.

Good enough.

Those were the words that Mum used.

Tally stares at the list, her eyes blurring. She might be all of these things but they aren't *her* words. And she needs her own words if she's going to do what Nell said and figure out who she actually is. She thinks back to the conversation she had with Mum in the kitchen, when Mum asked her what she'd done that made her feel proud. She remembers that day with Miles and Luke in the school hall and she thinks about the person that she was and suddenly, the word is right there, shining and dancing before her eyes.

Brave.

Tally is *brave* and she always tries to do the right thing, no matter how hard it might be.

Her hand swipes across the ground, scattering the words into dust. Her brain is fizzing and whirring, and the den suddenly feels too small for her and her thoughts. Maybe the den has shrunk since the last time she was in here or maybe she's grown, but, either way, it isn't the safe place that it used to be.

She doesn't want to write her words in the dirt – her words need room to move and stretch. Her words need to fly, not be tethered to the ground.

Scrabbling out of the den, she ducks under the willow branches and runs down the garden. The ladder is lying next to the garden shed and it takes all her strength to lift it up and rest it in position. She does it though – she's tenacious like that. Then she climbs up, one rung at a time, nearly losing her grip when she reaches the third rung that's almost rotted through, until she gets to the top.

Taking a deep breath, Tally clambers up the steep sides of the roof. And then she pulls one leg over so that she is straddling the ridge, sitting astride the rooftop with the ground far below her.

Not that she's interested in the world below right now. All of her attention is on the sky, the endless sky that goes on and on and on. A sky big enough to hold all of her words and give them space to grow.

Brave.

Tally releases her first word into the air where it glides on the breeze.

Fierce.

Exciting.

The words just keep on coming, like birds escaping a cage.

Loyal.

Adventurous.

Loving.

They float out in front of her and then rise on the current, ascending so high that they are almost out of sight before plunging back down to play.

And now there's only one word left. Tally cradles it in her hands like a tiny fledgling and then gently sends it into the air. It flaps its wings a little, as if it isn't really sure what it's supposed to be doing, and Tally holds her breath, certain that it's going to plummet to the ground.

Autistic.

And then, as she watches, it takes flight and soars into the sky to join the others, swooping and frolicking and flying free, and soon Tally can't distinguish it from the rest. All of her words, tangled together to make her who she is – the letters rearranging themselves to spell out the most important word of all.

Tally.

Nell was right (much as it pains her to admit it). She needs to make things right and she knows exactly how to do it.

And it starts by being proud to be her.

A word that helps me
Understand who I am and why I feel the way that I do.
Telling me that it's OK to be different, and that really,
I am more than just this word - or any other word you
can think of.
Same laugh, same smile, same voice.
Me.

When I first got my autism diagnosis, it kind of felt like a
weight was lifted off my shoulders, but was then replaced
by another even heavier one. Before, I just knew that
what I did was "different", but now I know why too.

Before the diagnosis, I was ashamed of myself and how I
behaved, and I've realized that when I got diagnosed and
found out that I can't help a lot of what I do, it was like
a sigh of relief. But at the same time, having it confirmed
that I really was "different" made me feel rubbish. I felt
like I had lost myself a bit and that I could never go
back. Before, I was someone - even if that someone had
troubles. And then suddenly I was nothing but a word.

But being treated differently can be good. Having
people understand what makes things difficult for you

and trying their hardest to meet your needs is actually pretty incredible. It does feel weird at first to be labelled with this word, but before that I was labelled with lots of words and none of them were right. At least now I have a word that is.

The very best thing about getting a diagnosis of autism is that I'm starting to understand myself better. For now I need to get used to it myself a bit more and that's OK. I know now that I'm not just one word, I'm lots of words and "autistic" is just one of them.

CHAPTER 26

Layla isn't waiting for Tally at the start of the day, and it takes every ounce of courage that Tally possesses to walk into the classroom alone. The room is bustling with noise and activity as everyone hangs up their costumes and chatters about their nerves, and Miss Balogun is racing from one part of the room to the other, shouting orders and ticking off items on her clipboard, but Layla is sitting alone at her desk, her face deep in thought.

"I'm sorry," says Tally, sliding into the seat next to her. "I shouldn't have taken the necklace and I'm going to make it better, but I need you to help me, OK?"

Layla glances up at her, with eyes that look sad.

"I didn't think you could ever do something so mean," she says quietly. "And I've never heard you tell a lie before either."

Tally shakes her head. "I didn't lie," she says hurriedly. "I just didn't tell the truth. And I didn't take it from her drawer – I just found it on the floor. Honestly."

Layla squints at her. "That's just as bad," she says. "Carrie was really upset about her lucky charm and you should have given it back."

Tally opens her mouth to explain. She knows that if she tells Layla about everything that's been going on – the appointment with Dr Zennor and the autism diagnosis – Layla will understand. She won't think that Tally is such a bad person any more.

But then she remembers what Mum told her yesterday. Autism is a reason but it's not an excuse.

"I know that now," she says. "And I really am sorry. Please will you help me to make it better? I've got a plan."

She will tell Layla because she's her best friend and she's always there for Tally, no matter what.

Just not today.

And not for the wrong reasons.

Layla looks at her, puzzled. "What plan?"

And so Tally leans in close and whispers her idea and the more she talks, the more that Layla smiles, and by the time she has finished explaining, her best friend's face is shining with excitement.

"So will you help?" repeats Tally.

"Of course I will!" Layla squeals, before clamping her hand to her mouth and glancing around guiltily to check that nobody heard. "This is going to be brilliant!"

"I need to talk to Miles as well." Tally stands up and grins at Layla. "If it's going to work then we need him to change the opening lights to make it as dramatic as possible."

"No *way*." Miles stares at Tally like she's suddenly grown horns. "You want me to change the opening light sequence with only four hours' notice?" He shakes his head. "It can't be done."

"It can," Tally assures him. "But only by you."

He stares at her for a moment and then stands up.

"Miss Balogun? I have to go and check the light board and I need Tally to come with me. Is that OK?"

There is a crash as Lucy drops a box of props and the teacher flinches.

"Do what you need to do," she calls distractedly before striding across to where Lucy is crouching on the floor. "Is anything broken? Please tell me that Grandmother's glasses are still in one piece?"

Miles grabs hold of Tally's hand, whisking her out of

the room and down the stairs, not releasing her until they're safely in the privacy of the hall.

"Tell me what's going on," he demands.

"Just sort the lights," begs Tally. "*Please*."

"I'll sort the lights when you've told me why." Miles plants his feet firmly on the floor. "Has this got something to do with Carrie's lucky charm?"

Tally's head snaps up, and she gazes at him in shock.

"What do you know about that?" she murmurs. "*How* do you know about that?"

Miles pushes his glasses up his nose and bends over the light board. "It was obvious. You kept going on and on about needing good luck and then all of a sudden you got the part in the production and Carrie was off sick. It was easy to deduce that you had the necklace and that it was giving you all the luck."

Tally's mouth drops open and Miles glances up at her with laughing eyes.

"I'm kidding," he tells her, sniggering quietly. "I told you – I don't believe in luck."

"So how did you know?" Tally asks him.

"You just told me, didn't you?" Miles smirks and looks back at the light board. "And besides, you're always getting it out of your pocket. I'm just surprised nobody else spotted it. You're not very cunning."

"Do you think I'm horrible?" Tally's voice is quiet.

Miles shakes his head. "No."

"Shall I tell you why I took it?"

He shakes his head even harder. "I guess you had a good reason. Now – tell me what I'm supposed to be doing and why."

Tally blinks and tries to focus.

"I'm going to make it better," she says. "And I need you to make the opening lights as dramatic as you possibly can. Look – I'll show you."

Tally runs across the hall and up the small steps to the stage.

"At the moment, the lights are already on when Little Red enters the stage," she calls. "But I want you to change that. Let her come on while it's still dark."

"OK." Miles lowers a lever and the stage is plunged into darkness.

"And then, after a few moments of waiting, to really get the audience's attention – boom! A single spotlight."

"Right. Like this?"

Miles flips a switch and a strong beam of light shoots down from the ceiling, making a golden puddle on the wooden stage. And in the middle of the light, there is

Tally, her arms spread wide and a huge grin on her face.

"That's perfect," she breathes. "Can you do that again later?"

Miles scribbles some notes on his lighting plan and makes a huffing noise. "It's going to mess up the next sequence," he mutters. "I'm going to have to reconfigure the whole first act. But I can do it."

He flicks the room into brightness again and Tally looks down at him.

"But *will* you do it?" she asks. "Please will you do it?"

He nods and she leaps off the stage, coming to join him at the lighting desk.

"You know next year, when we're at Kingswood Academy?" she says. "They have a massive drama department and an entire room just for the technical stuff. I've been going for extra visits so that I can get used to what it all looks like, and they showed us the stage and everything on our last trip. We met the drama teacher too – her name is Mrs Jarman and she's a bit scary but there's something good about her. You're going to love it there!"

Miles puts down his pencil and looks over Tally's shoulder.

"I'm not going to that school," he tells her. "I'm going somewhere else. Somewhere a bit smaller. My parents think I might find it easier to make some friends there."

Tally's stomach flips over, like a pancake.

"I thought you weren't that bothered about friends," she says. "You told me that you didn't want to fit in and be like everyone else."

Miles smiles at the floor. "I don't. But that doesn't mean that I don't want friends. Now – I need to figure out how to change the lights so that you can have your dramatic entrance, and you need to go and get your costume sorted. You're going to shine like a star, Tally – and I'll help you."

She could tell him that the light isn't for her. Or she could leave it as a surprise, just like it's going to be for everyone else.

"Thank you for helping me." Tally takes a step towards the door. "You're a good friend, Miles. I think you're going to make lots of new friends at your new school."

And then she's gone, back up to the classroom where Layla is waiting to put the finishing touches to their plan into action.

CHAPTER 27

The morning is over and lunchtime has gone and it's time. The boys' costumes are hanging at the edge of the stage while the girls get changed in the small room off to one side. The air is fizzing with excitement and nerves and the occasional squeal of delight as someone peeps out of the door to spot the hall filling up with the audience.

"I can see my mum!" calls Jasmine. "And your parents too, Carrie. They're sitting together."

"I told them not to come," murmurs Carrie. "It's not like I'm actually doing anything. Miles won't let me touch his light board, and the only job I have is to turn the pages of his script. It's very boring."

"Are you all dressed?" Miss Balogun walks into the room. "Tally! Why aren't you in your costume?"

"It's gone missing," Tally tells her. "I can't find it anywhere."

Miss Balogun's face turns a strange shade of pink and she sucks in a loud breath. "It can't have just disappeared," she groans. "You need to find it. Now!"

"I'll help her, Miss," says Layla and the teacher nods.

"You've got two minutes and then you'll have to go on in your school uniform," she threatens, before ushering everyone else out and into their places at the side of the stage, out of sight of the waiting audience.

And then there are only three people left.

Tally. Layla. Carrie.

The moment has arrived.

"Quick!" Tally turns to Layla, who races into the corner of the room and drags the Little Red costume out from behind a pile of boxes. "Now put it on!"

She thrusts the costume into Carrie's hands. The other girl stares at it for a moment and then looks up at Tally and Layla.

"How did it get there?" she asks. "And why do you want me to put it on?"

"Just hurry up!" cries Tally. "You heard Miss Balogun – we've got two minutes!"

"We hid it there earlier," says Layla, seeing that Carrie

is clearly in need of an explanation. "So that there would be time for Tally to surprise you."

"Surprise me?" says Carrie weakly.

Tally tries to suppress her irritation but really, Carrie is being remarkably slow, and if the plan is going to work then she hasn't got time to go into everything.

"I'm choosing you to play the part of Little Red," she says, gesturing towards the costume. "You get to go on stage after all."

In her head, the moment after this big reveal was wonderful. Carrie would exclaim with delight and tell Tally that she was a truly fantastic person and that she couldn't believe anyone could be so kind. And she'd have made everything better and it would be worth the sacrifice of relinquishing the part.

The reality is slightly different. Carrie's eyes narrow and she isn't smiling with joy. Instead she is scowling at Tally as if she has never heard anything so terrible in all her life.

"Surprise…!" tries Tally, in an attempt to get things back on the right track. "Surprise…?"

"Why are you only telling me now?" Carrie's voice is unimpressed. "Why did you wait until the absolute final moment?"

Tally shrugs. "I wasn't sure if I could choose for it to be you, but now I know. So I'm telling you."

"You could have mentioned it earlier." Carrie is looking at Layla now, who is shuffling awkwardly from one foot to the other.

Layla nods apologetically. "It sounded more exciting this way," she says. "And at least you get to play the part of Little Red."

Carrie frowns. "No way. I can't just go on stage now. I haven't had a chance to get ready or prepare." She looks at Tally. "You'll have to do it."

The three girls stand in silence, staring at each other with none of them sure what to do next. And then the door flies open and Miss Balogun is striding into the room.

"Oh, thank goodness!" she exclaims, spying the costume in Carrie's hands. "You found it. But why aren't you wearing it, Tally?"

"I want Carrie to play Little Red," says Tally.

"I can't do it," argues Carrie. "It has to be you."

Miss Balogun holds her hand up to stop anyone saying anything further.

"At this point I don't care who puts on the costume," she barks. "But one of you had better be out on that stage in exactly two minutes. Layla! Get into position please."

Layla shoots an anxious look at Tally before scurrying out after the harassed teacher. Once the door is closed, Tally turns to face Carrie one more time.

"You have to go on," she tells her. "It's your part really."

Carrie's eyes flood with tears. "I'm too scared," she confesses. "Please, Tally. I can't do it. I need you to step in and be Little Red. I've got horrible stage fright – there's no way that I can go on."

And for one, glorious moment, Tally can see how it can all work out for the best. She did the right thing and offered the part to Carrie, but if she's got stage fright then there's nothing for it but for Tally to save the day – and the part will rightfully be hers because Carrie is *asking* her to help. She can do the right thing for Carrie and still show everyone just what she is capable of achieving when she puts her mind to it. She can dazzle them all with her acting and everybody will think she is a hero.

It's not like there are any other options, after all. She's tried telling Carrie that the part is hers and she hasn't got any other way of coaxing the other girl on to the stage. But someone has to do it and she knows that she can be brilliant.

"OK." She takes the costume out of Carrie's hands and starts to pull off her cardigan. "If you're sure."

And then she stops.

Because there *is* one more thing that she can do, even though the very thought of it makes her feel a bit sick. Miles told her that she was going to shine like a star, and if she's going to do that then…

She has to own up to her mistakes.

"You *can* go on," she says firmly, shoving the costume at Carrie and yanking her arm back into the sleeve of her cardigan. "You're a fantastic singer and a great actor, and you don't need to be nervous. But just in case you need it, you'd better have this back."

She rams her hand into her pocket and pulls out the ladybird necklace. Carrie gawps at her and then reaches out slowly, picking up the lucky charm and holding it in the palm of her hand.

"I found it," says Tally in a hurry. "And I kept it because I wanted to be as lucky as you are. And I'm sorry about that, because it was the wrong thing to do. But it didn't work for me anyway, and that's OK because, actually, I don't think that I believe in luck." Carrie's face falls and Tally quickly backtracks. "I don't believe in luck for *me*, I mean. I totally believe in luck for *you*!"

"I can't believe you've had it this whole time," mutters Carrie, still staring at Tally. "Or that you think I'm lucky.

Why would you think that?"

"It all looks easy for you," says Tally, shrugging. "But I shouldn't have kept it."

"You've got thirty seconds," bellows Miss Balogun from the other side of the door. "And then I'm cancelling the entire thing if one of you isn't out here in that costume."

"Good luck," says Tally. "And I *am* sorry. I didn't mean to make you sad."

Carrie looks again at the lucky charm in her hand and then flashes Tally a small smile.

"Why did you own up?" she asks, starting to pull the costume over her head. "I'd never have known it was you that took it."

"*I'd* have known," Tally tells her, and then she leaves the room and makes her way to the lighting desk, where Miles is waiting anxiously for the cue to start.

"*What are you doing here?*" he hisses, as Tally slips into the seat next to his. "You're supposed to be *up there!*"

Miss Balogun appears at the side of the stage and gives Miles a wave. He glances at Tally and she nods, and even though she knows that he doesn't get it, he follows their plan. The stage remains in darkness as the music starts to play and at the edge of Tally's vision she can see Miss Balogun starting to stalk towards them, not understanding why the lights aren't yet on.

"Now," she whispers, as the teacher is almost at the desk. "Do it now."

Miles flips the switch and a single spotlight glows in the darkness, lighting up the girl on the stage. The audience gasps and Carrie starts to sing, and across the hall, Mum turns to give Tally the proudest smile she has ever seen.

"You were supposed to be the star," Miles mutters as the audience applauds Carrie's song and Luke prowls on to the stage in his wolf costume.

Tally just grins at him and turns the page of his script.

She could tell him that you can still be a star, even when you're hidden in the depths of the shadows and, actually, if you really think about it, stars always shine their brightest when everything else is at its darkest.

But some things you just have to find out for yourself.

WHO IS TALLY?

A legend. Only joking, but I'm not your average ten-year-old. I used to want to be, but now I don't mind being different.

WHY SHOULD TALLY BE YOUR FAVOURITE PERSON EVER?

Because I am brave, strong, autistic and I'm learning to believe in myself so I think you should too! I'm also getting tall, and am the tallest in my class actually.

MY FAVOURITE MOTTO:

Be yourself; everybody else is taken.

CHAPTER 28

Tally stares at the bowl in front of her and tries to stay calm.

"But I don't understand," says Dad, his voice exasperated. "You used to love tomato soup. What's wrong with it?"

The simple answer to his question is *everything*, but Tally knows that he won't get it. And she wants him to understand, she really does. She needs him to know that she isn't being naughty or difficult or fussy. She needs him to know that she can't help how the bowl in front of her is making her feel.

"Is it the colour?" asks Mum, trying to be helpful.

Tally nods. The colour is one of the problems. Red is the colour of anger and explosion and STOP, and she doesn't want to put any of that in her mouth.

"Is it the texture?" continues Mum. She and Dad have been on a course for parents of autistic children, and Tally can always tell when she's trying out one of the strategies that they have suggested. It makes her feel cross – they keep on telling her how unique she is, but then try to use tactics that work with other kids. Sometimes when Mum uses this stuff, Tally pretends that it doesn't work, even when the ideas are quite good. She isn't *other kids* and she can't just be put into a special "autistic" box.

She ignores Mum but the texture *is* a problem. It's smooth and silky and the thought that there could be a rogue tomato lump lurking in the murky depths makes her stomach turn.

"Has anyone thought that it might just be the taste?" Nell rolls her eyes at Tally. "Because I don't know about you, but I think it tastes like wet cardboard."

Tally feels a giggle bubble up inside her, but it is quickly squashed when Dad sighs heavily and puts his spoon down loudly on the table.

"I've had quite enough of this," he says. "I've cooked us all a delicious lunch and everyone just needs to stop talking and eat up."

Tally's head starts to fizz. Mum and Dad have learnt

a ton of stuff on their course, but they still don't seem to understand how it makes her feel when they order her about.

So tell them.

She glances around, but Dad is picking up his spoon and Mum has a mouthful of soup and Nell is busy cutting a piece of toast into small strips. None of them are looking at her and none of them are talking.

Be brave, Tally. Try to tell them.

She swallows hard and takes a deep breath. How can she tell them when her throat is closed up and her stomach is whirling? How can she tell them when the words won't come out of her mouth?

She picks up the bowl and holds it in her hands, careful not to spill a single drop. She might not have the words to tell them, but she can show them and then they might understand that no matter what they say, she cannot eat this soup.

"Tally." Mum's voice is quiet and calm.

She looks up and sees Mum and Nell looking at her while Dad's eyes dart frantically between her and the pristine kitchen wall that he spent all of last Sunday painting.

"Talk to me, lovely girl." Mum keeps on trying, but it

doesn't matter how gently she says it, Tally can't get the words out of her mouth. Maybe if she was sitting on top of the shed roof then they'd be able to fly free but here, in the house, they're imprisoned in her head.

She takes aim. The red soup is going to look kind of amazing dripping down the white wall.

"Maybe you can write down how you're feeling." Mum's words push through the buzzing in Tally's head. "If you can't tell us, maybe you can write it down. Some people find that writing in a journal can really help them figure out their thoughts, so I got you this."

Tally blinks away the red and looks at Mum, who is getting up and walking across to open one of the kitchen drawers. She pulls out a book and then brings it back to the table, holding it in front of Tally.

"It's a diary," she tells her. "And it's just for you. You can write in it – but only if you want to, and it's not for anyone else to read."

"Why?" Tally lowers the bowl of soup and pretends not to hear Dad's sigh of relief. "What am I supposed to write?"

Mum looks at her. "You can write whatever you want to write. How you're feeling or what you've been doing or your hopes and dreams for the future." She laughs. "It's the book of *you*."

"So the whole thing is about me?" asks Tally, taking the diary from Mum and turning it over in her hands. "And I can write anything in it? Anything at all?"

"Yes," confirms Mum, picking up her spoon.

"Can I write about what it's like to be autistic?" Tally opens the first page and sees a clean, blank page. "Can I write about who I really am?"

"You can." Mum smiles, a little secret smile, like she's feeling warm inside. "So, do you think you might like to use it?"

Tally pushes the bowl away and picks up a piece of toast. Later on she can tell her new diary all about how it makes her feel when people try to make her do things that upset her or scare her or make her feel worried, but right now her stomach is growling and she wants to eat her lunch.

"I might," she says, putting the diary carefully on to the table. "Maybe. If I feel like it."

Mum nods and starts talking to Nell about her plans for the afternoon. Dad keeps eating his soup, pausing now and then to join in with their conversation. And Tally munches her toast and gazes at her diary. She has big plans for this journal and she likes the idea of having her own way to figure out who she really is and helping other people to see her too.

She's going to write the book of *her*.

And it's going to be wild and fierce and real, and all the amazing, wonderful things that she is. Because if she knows only one thing, it's that there are lots of ways to be her and every single one of them is special.

LIBBY'S TOP TIPS ON HOW TO BE
FRIENDS WITH AN AUTISTIC PERSON

1. Understand that while many of us don't like being in new or uncomfortable social situations, this does not mean we don't like being sociable. We might just struggle to handle the awkwardness that some social situations bring. It's always a relief if someone approaches me and strikes up a conversation, as I just can't cope with starting that kind of small talk myself. Bear with me if I seem unfriendly or aloof at the beginning. It's just because I'm feeling awkward and I hate that I come across like that. I want to be one of those warm sunny people that makes friends easily, but I'm just not. Yet. Maybe I never will be and that's OK.

2. Don't treat us like an alien species. We simply experience the world a bit differently from you. Take all the thoughts that come into your head when you hear the word autistic and throw most of them in the bin because that's where they probably belong. Learn about that person as an individual, not what

you think the word autism means. Some of us have learning difficulties, some of us don't. Some of us find it really easy to learn super complex stuff. Some of us don't. Some of us talk a lot, some of us don't. Some of us love hanging out with others, some of us don't. Even when it comes to things like sensory differences, special interests, and so on, we may share similar traits, but we all experience them in different ways.

3. Ask us what we need. We may have our difficulties at times, but the best way to make an autistic person feel comfortable is to do your best to understand them and what they need. If you make this effort and maybe adapt a little, we can shine and be the best kind of friend.

4. Dive below the surface. This is a really difficult one I know, but if your autistic friend seems difficult or argumentative, then instead of getting caught up in it, try not to judge them but to understand that is not really them, it's just how they are feeling at that moment. They may be feeling anxious about something or really stressed by something – it could

be anything from the lights being too bright to someone having said something unpleasant to them. Instead of responding with anger, try to respond with a question like "Hey, what's up? You seem like you're having a hard time about something."

5. Look in another direction while you are talking to your autistic friend so that they don't feel under pressure to look at your face and make eye contact. That way they will feel so relaxed and they will be able to listen better.

6. Word things differently, or say them in a gentler tone of voice. Many of us are really sensitive and get carried along by our feelings. Some comments that may just wash off other people can stick with us for days and days. We may be going over something you said or we did for hours and hours every night when it is long forgotten for you. So a little bit of care and thought in the first place, even though I know it's difficult, can make a massive difference to how we end up thinking and feeling.

7. Get interested in what we love. Most autistic people

have some kind of special interest. One of mine is - you've guessed it - Taylor Swift. Another one is animals. I just adore them, and it may come across as annoying if I keep going on about them, but try to embrace it and just go with it - it's part of who I am. Find out what your autistic friend loves most of all and ask them questions about it, send them pictures or interesting articles about it, and most of all - let them talk to you about it and actually listen and genuinely show interest. This is one of the best gifts you can give an autistic person - honestly, nothing will make them happier!

8. Never ever use the word autistic as an insult. Just don't.

9. That extra bit of kindness can go a long way with an autistic person. I think because we are often being told how frustrating or difficult or annoying we are, it makes such a lovely change to hear good things about ourselves. Telling us something you really like about us, or how we make you feel good, or praising us for something we do well. Just really being warm and friendly and positive with us can really bring us out of

our shell, but only if it's genuine. We can spot a fake a mile off.

10. Look for the treasure. When you spend time connecting with an autistic person, you can help to clear their mind of all the negative stuff that has been fed in and built up over time from people who aren't so kind. Imagine you are clearing out a basement that's full of junk. As you clear away the rubbish that's built up there over the years, then you just might find something wonderful, something precious and special like treasure. My treasure is that I have a really sharp sense of humour and can say the funniest things when I feel relaxed and liked. My mum says that no one makes her laugh like I do. And that makes me feel on top of the world.

ACKNOWLEDGEMENTS

Libby would like to thank her mum, dad and sister for loving and supporting her. Special thanks to Vicky, Adam, Marnie and Frankie for being the best neighbours ever and helping her get through lockdowns with laughter.

Finally a big thank you to the girls at her new school who have welcomed her so warmly and taken the time to understand her.

Rebecca would like to thank her fabulous family – Adam, Zach, Gee and Reuben. No matter how challenging the times or dark the days, you are always there – ready to step up and make things better. You are all incredible and I love you very much.

Also a big thank you to Polly and Elsie Couldrick for reading an early draft and giving their advice.

Libby and I are so lucky that we get to work together, with the expert support of our agent, Julia Churchill, our editor, Fiz Osborne and Libby's amazing mum, Kym Scott. Who'd have thought that a single tweet could lead to the creation of three wonderful books?!

READ ON FOR AN EXTRACT OF
CAN YOU SEE ME?

People think that because Tally's autistic, she doesn't realize what they're thinking, but Tally sees and hears – and notices – all of it. Endearing, insightful and warmly uplifting, this is a story of autism, empathy and kindness that will touch readers of all ages.

CHAPTER 1

Look up. Go on, do it now. Stretch back your neck and stare up, as far as you can. And then a little bit more. That's where you're going to have to look if you want to find Tally Olivia Adams. Up where the sky begins. Up where the only rule is gravity. Up where the world seems small and not so important. Up where the possibilities are endless.

It is a final-days-of-summer kind of afternoon. Fluffy white clouds are scudding across the pale blue sky and the air has a hint of something fresh, something new. A normal day on a normal street in the back garden of a normal house belonging to a completely normal family. Read that last sentence again, out loud to yourself. It's funny how if you say it enough times, the word normal sounds anything but.

So, a normal day. But the girl standing on the roof of the garden shed is not normal in the slightest. She is a warrior, fierce and brave, surveying the land before her. She's a mountain climber, pausing for breath after scaling the heady heights of Everest. She is a trapeze artist, about to step out on to the wire and dazzle the crowds beneath her.

Her right foot rises in the air, shaking slightly as she contemplates the drop. One wrong move and it will all be over.

"Hey! Get down!"

The shout makes Tally wobble and for a split second it seems as if she will tumble to earth. But then her foot makes contact with the roof and she lowers herself to the ridge, sitting with her legs dangling out in front of her.

"You nearly made me fall." Tally glares at Nell accusingly. "Are you trying to kill me?"

Nell puts her hands on her hips. "You seem to be doing a good enough job of that by yourself. What are you doing? You know Mum and Dad said that you aren't allowed to go up there any more. Not after last time."

Tally shrugs. "It's my place. I'm practising the things I learnt in circus school last week. And I can't think anywhere else."

"It's the holidays." Nell taps her foot impatiently. "There isn't anything *to* think about, so just get down."

Tally wonders if her sister has always been this unimaginative or if it's something that happens when you start high school. If that's the case then she's even less keen for this week to be over and September to begin.

"Is it true that people flush your head down the toilet when you're in year seven?" she asks Nell. "Because if it is then I won't be able to drink anything all day in case it makes me need to use the bathroom, which means that I will be seriously dehydrated and my brain won't work very effectively and I'm probably going to fail every single test. And it won't even be my fault because all I'll be trying to do is stay as far away from the school toilets as humanly possible."

Nell snorts. "Only the mouthy kids that don't know when to shut up."

A warm breeze flutters through the garden, picking up the leaves that have fallen on to the lawn. They weren't there last week and their russet-red shine against the long, green grass is a reminder that the summer can't last for ever. Her days at home are numbered.

"What happens if I get lost?" Tally's voice is quiet.

Nell pushes her hair out of her eyes and squints up at the roof.

"Then the two-headed monster that lives in the caretaker's cupboard will find you," she says, as menacingly as she possibly can. "And it will drag you in and keep you hostage amongst the brooms and mops and buckets. And you will have to stay at school for the rest of your life."

Tally doesn't even blink. She isn't afraid of made-up monsters. There are far scarier things roaming the school corridors than two-headed beasts, she's quite sure of that.

"Come on, Tally." Nell is impatient now. "Get down from there. I'm totally not in the mood for Mum and Dad giving me another lecture about how I should be keeping an eye on you. Like you're some kind of baby or something."

"I'm not a baby. And I didn't ask you to come out here." Tally glares down at Nell. "Just go away and pretend that you didn't see me."

"Well, you're lucky it was me that caught you and not them." Nell frowns, imagining the argument that would have followed if her parents had spotted their youngest daughter on top of the shed.

Tally shakes her head. She doesn't feel very lucky to have moaning, nagging, boring Nell ruining her thinking time.

"You'll be grounded for a week if they see you up there," warns Nell. "They won't even let you into the garden if they think they can't trust you."

Tally looks away from her big sister and across the garden fence towards the street. She knows that if she stands up, she can see between the houses and as far as the park. She can see further than Nell can. Up here she is weightless and free. The opposite of grounded.

"Where are they?" she asks Nell. "Mum and Dad."

Nell glances back towards the house, which is almost hidden by the old apple tree, sagging under the weight of all the unpicked fruit. The entire garden has turned into a jungle this summer.

"They're out by the front gate, talking to Mrs Jessop and her gross dog," she tells Tally. "I don't know how she can take it for walks when it looks like that. It's embarrassing."

"It's not Rupert's fault that he's got three legs." Tally is unimpressed with Nell's attitude. "Don't be so horrible. Think about how you'd feel if you had three legs. You wouldn't like it if people thought you looked gross, would you?"

Nell rolls her eyes. "Whatever. But I wouldn't go outside either. I wouldn't force other people to look at my freakiness. Now get down before they come out here and see you."

She waits for a response but Tally isn't listening. Instead, she is clambering to her feet and balancing on the roof, shading her eyes with one hand as she peers into the distance.

"I think there's a fair going up in the park. There's a load of people and caravans and I can see a big truck that looks like it has dodgem cars on the back."

"What?" Nell squints up at Tally. "That can't be right. The fair isn't coming for months yet. And will you please get down before you fall off and I get the blame?"

"I'm not going to fall off. And I *can* see the fair, actually."

"Are you sure?" Nell strains to stand on her tiptoes and look in the direction of the park, but she can't see a thing.

The fair is one of the few things that they both agree is a *good thing*. It doesn't matter that Nell is fourteen and Tally is only eleven – when the fair is in town they are both as excited as each other.

Tally plants her feet more firmly and leans forward, trying to identify the different lorries and vans. "I think I can see the Twirler. And there's something that could be part of the carousel – it looks like one of the horses, anyway!"

There's the sound of scrambling beneath her and suddenly Nell's head pops up from the top of the ladder.

"Where? Are you sure it's actually setting up in our park?" Her voice is eager with an added tinge of apprehension. This wouldn't be the first time that Tally has got things wrong.

"See for yourself." Tally waves her hand towards the distance. "If you don't believe me."

There's a moment of hesitation and then Nell climbs the last few rungs and crawls her way up the roof to where Tally is standing.

"I still can't see anything."

"I can see the haunted house!" Tally looks down at Nell, a huge beaming smile spreading across her face. "I really can!"

It's too much for Nell. She pulls herself to her feet and balances alongside Tally on the ridge of the shed, her hand reaching out and gripping Tally's so tightly that the blood throbs and hums in her fingers.

"You're right! It *is* the fair!"

"I told you." Tally doesn't mind her sister's lack of faith. She knew that she was right all along.

Together, they watch as the lorries are opened and machinery is pulled out and assembled. It's almost magic, the way that the ordinary, clunky bits of metal fit together to create something brilliant.

"I'm sorry that I was being stupid about you starting in year seven," murmurs Nell. "You don't need to worry, Tally. I'll be right there if you need me, and it's not that scary. Nobody is going to flush your head down the toilet, I promise. You'll be fine – school is way less frightening than the haunted house and you can handle that!"

Tally doesn't reply because this is a very ignorant thing for Nell to have said and, sometimes, ignorant comments are best ignored. You can't compare the haunted house to Kingswood Academy. It just doesn't work.

The haunted house is Tally and Nell's thing and they always go together. Tally loves the delicious thrill of the spooky music and weird sound effects and the way that, no matter how many times she's been on the ride, she always jumps in her seat when the sinister, rattling skeleton lurches out at them towards the end. But most of all, she loves the rules that are written down on the board at the entrance.

Do not get out of the carriage.

Keep your hands inside the carriage.

Do not eat or drink on the ride.

Tally doesn't usually like rules, especially if they've come from other people, but these rules are different. They feel helpful and they keep her safe. And anyway, the haunted house is just pretend.

But Kingswood Academy is real. And she knows that while there are plenty of rules, the ones that really matter aren't written down anywhere.

"We have to persuade Mum and Dad to let us go to the fair," says Nell, squeezing Tally's hand. "We have to. Which means that we can't let them find us up here."

And because Tally wants to go to the fair just as much as Nell does, she lets her sister pull her towards the ladder and back to solid ground.

Date: Friday 29th August.

Situation: the summer holidays.

How I feel: relaxed but a bit nervous – the summer can't last for ever, can it?

Anxiety rating: A nice, chilled-out 3 with a hint of 4 creeping in if I think about starting in year seven next week.

Dear Diary,

Tally here. Well, I'm actually Natalia but my friends call me Tally, and so do my family. Let me tell you about my family! I live with my mum, Jennifer, my dad, Kevin, and my annoying big sister, Nell. She thinks she's always right, and even when she is I pretend that she isn't.

Mum's given me this diary so that I can write down how I'm feeling. She says that it might help me to understand how I cope (or don't cope) in different situations, particularly when I get anxious or scared (which happens a lot, by the way).

One thing that you should probably know about me early on is that I'm autistic. I have autism.

Although autism can sometimes hold me up a little in life, my parents say it's a superpower, and I like to believe that. The rest of the world hasn't caught up with us yet, though, and some people seem to think that being autistic is like being a different species. Some people treat me like an alien when all I want is to be treated like any other eleven-year-old. I'll admit that what also sometimes makes people treat me differently is the fact that I wear a tiger mask a lot of the time. I just feel secure and safe in it. When I'm wearing my mask, I don't have to make eye contact (why are people SO obsessed with this anyway?), or pretend to smile at people. I can't catch germs in it and people tend to leave me alone when I'm wearing it. What's not to love? Though, Nell doesn't love it. She finds it excruciatingly embarrassing when I wear it in public. She even tried to hide it once. The mask is Nell's arch enemy. And I like that. *evil laugh*.

There are some things I think people should know about my autism. Let's call them autism pros and cons. I'm going to write them down in my diary as I think of them. (One day I'm going to share these with the world so they can see autism from another perspective.)

Tally's autism facts: Sensory stuff

Pro: I have better memory, sense of smell, eyesight,

sense of touch, hearing and sometimes taste than others might. (I told you that autism is a superpower!) I can hear a piece of music and play it instantly on my keyboard or ukulele, I can mimic voices (which I sometimes get into trouble for), and I can remember where and when we bought every one of my soft toys (and I have over a hundred of them). I usually remember to celebrate all of their birthdays, too, except that time I forgot Billy's (I was devastated).

Con: I can feel even the tiniest of things and it annoys the hell out of me. Seams in socks, a crumb in my shoe, labels in clothes. If we go on holiday and the mattress isn't exactly like my one at home, I can't sleep for feeling the lumps. Mum says I'm just like the Princess in the Princess and the Pea story. Having excellent hearing isn't always so great. It makes it impossible to block out other people's conversations even when I'm all the way upstairs in my bedroom. And when that conversation is Mum and Dad having an argument about me then it's even worse (yet also intriguing I have to admit). But when I let on that I've heard, I get accused of eavesdropping, which is disgraceful really, considering I can't help it.

ALSO AVAILABLE FROM LIBBY SCOTT AND REBECCA WESTCOTT

Tally is autistic and proud. She used to feel that she had to hide her autism, but now Tally is determined to make sure people see who she really is. Except for one thing - Tally's school trip, which means new places, new people and new challenges.